THE WRONG BROTHER

Captain Rhodes kept his distance, but Madeline caught his gaze on her each time she glanced in his direction, which was often. She knew enough about gentlemen to recognize when one was interested in her. She desperately wanted his attention and felt guilty for the wanting. It would never do. She could not care for one brother while pretending to consider the betrothal of the other.

Prompted by some demon of mischief, she flirted outrageously with each of her admirers in turn. From under her hat, she tossed them looks that gave the impression she had eyes for them alone.

At sixteen, she had behaved this way when the young guardsmen of Point Henry had noticed her. But with Captain Titus Rhodes, it was different.

What was there about him that made her behave in such a forward way?

AN INNOCENT RUSE

MARY MORROW

HarperPaperbacks
A Division of HarperCollinsPublishers

This is a work of fiction. The characters, incidents, and
dialogues are products of the author's imagination and are not
to be construed as real. Any resemblance to actual events or
persons, living or dead, is entirely coincidental.

HarperPaperbacks   *A Division of* HarperCollins*Publishers*
                    10 East 53rd Street, New York, N.Y. 10022

Copyright © 1995 by Mary J. Morrow
All rights reserved. No part of this book may be used or
reproduced in any manner whatsoever without written
permission of the publisher, except in the case of brief
quotations embodied in critical articles and reviews. For
information address HarperCollins*Publishers,*
10 East 53rd Street, New York, N.Y. 10022.

Cover illustration by Rick Johnson

First HarperPaperbacks printing: August 1995

Printed in the United States of America

HarperPaperbacks, HarperMonogram, and colophon are
trademarks of HarperCollins*Publishers*

❖ 10 9 8 7 6 5 4 3 2 1

AN INNOCENT RUSE

1

The whole of Upper Canada still mourned its heroes.

Madeline Rose Smythe wept once more for her father, a revered and respected army officer, wounded when the Americans attacked Kingston Harbour and the Royal Naval Dockyard early in the dreadful War of 1812. The treaty ending the fierce commercial struggle was signed on Christmas Eve, 1814. Now with spring, she could finally keep her promise.

On this, her last day on Canadian soil, Madeline chose to wait where her family lay buried in the new cemetery overlooking Point Henry. She knelt before the two mounds, the stinging wind drying the tears on her cheeks. Her mother's grave had a stone with her name chiseled on it, Hilda Esmere

Smythe. Madeline remembered her as a laughing and gentle mama, a small woman of beauty and grace. She'd taught Madeline to behave in the refined manner of a lady. "For you are," she'd claimed in her soft voice. Papa would nod and insist Madeline pay close attention when Mama spoke of her family in far off England.

A flat rock marked her father's plot, the name and dates painted on with blacking that would soon wash away with the rains. Colonel Randall Smythe had confessed to Madeline of his regret in taking Mama from England. "We were so young and in love, Maddie. We thought love all that was necessary to succeed in life."

Marching boots echoed from the log fort on Point Henry, the sergeant's command sharp on the morning air as Madeline recalled her father's words. "My sweet daughter," he had said before closing his eyes for his last sleep. "You must go home to England. Your great-grandfather, a fine gentleman farmer, waits there for you. He understood about us, Hilda and I. But he warned me how it would be."

Madeline had ached for her proud officer father while she watched his weak efforts. Each day his strength had dwindled.

"Your great-grandfather writes that he is old and tired, but he cannot die until he lays eyes on his favorite granddaughter's only child." He'd labored to breathe, his voice but a whisper. "Promise me you'll go, without delay."

"I promise, Papa," was all she could manage, for the reality of losing her papa crushed her heart.

He'd died two hours later in his sleep, and Madeline had remained by his bedside until the army doctor from the fort led her away. Madeline believed if Mama had been alive, he would have fought harder to live.

Even if she had not made the promise, she could not remain in Canada; her position was too shaky. She no longer had a link with the British army and the general could not provide her with a residence.

This was a wild land of rough colonials who led coarse lives. As an unprotected female of twenty-four, she might be safe for a time, but she could not take the chance, for there was Esther to consider, too. Ruthless pillaging, rape, even murder lurked in the outer forests edging the town, albeit there were more good people here than bad. The settlers owned their own land and were subject to no master. The British army was the major law enforcement, but the guardsmen were too busy worrying about the aftermath of the battles to undertake domestic disputes.

Throughout the last two years, the construction of a considerable fortress at Point Henry had been underway. There were rumors of a proposed canal involving the Rideau and Cataraqui Rivers. It was all the talk. A canal was needed, it was said, and the British Royal Engineers were expected to construct it. In the event of another war between the United States and Britain, a safe escapeway to the interior of Upper Canada was imperative.

Only now, as the ice floes floated on the lake, would the general give permission for her journey from the protection of the garrison. He warned that even though the news of the treaty signing had surely penetrated the American strongholds, the trip through the United States territory could still be a dangerous one for a British sympathizer.

Rows of graves surrounded her; narrow resting places of guardsmen, many younger than she, who had fallen at the American attack. She swiped at fresh tears, for some of the men at one time or another had been her friends, or beaux.

From this hillside she could see the harbour, the landing wharf, Point Henry, the muddy streets of Kingston, and the vast forest bare of green save for the tall pines. Those same dark pines, wind-stripped of branches on their northern sides, reminded her of the staunch settlers she had lived beside all her life. She considered herself a Canadian, and she understood why despite harsh conditions, they refused to relinquish their new land.

Soon it would be time to travel across the lake and down the Mohawk and Hudson Rivers to the southern shore of New York. From there she would sail the Atlantic for England, and see for the first time the land of her birth, the homeland of her beloved parents.

Madeline kissed the palms of her hands and lay them on the mounds where her mama and papa rested.

Standing, she blew kisses east and west, the wind scattering them over her memory of upright soldiers in parade, their scarlet and gilt-edged jackets heralding untold bravery.

Gathering her heavy cape, she trudged out of the cemetery, down to the stepping rocks placed across the muddy track where Esther waited. She looked back, but the plots were hidden. She was alone now.

Madeline took the maid's hand and they squished through the mud to the jetty where they would board the schooner.

At the wharf Madeline smiled and hugged Esther's thin shoulders. "The clouds are gone. Look at the sun on the water." Gray-green swells lapped the rough planks, but beyond, the lake shone like a mirror with tiny diamonds floating on its surface. "A sure sign of sparkling tomorrows."

On a June morning, a special carrier delivered a letter from Lady Francesca Brock Rowe, London, to Esmere Grange, Leaside, in Devonshire, informing the occupants of the house that Miss Madeline Rose Smythe's arrival was imminent. A missive from such a society leader as Lady Rowe threw Lady Esmere into emotional agitation. The wife of the fifth Baron Esmere had grandiose visions of herself in the breast of society, if and when she could manipulate her husband into finalizing the purchase of a magnificent town house in the Mayfair district of London. Relations with the smart set were uppermost in Lady Esmere's thoughts. Forthwith, by teatime on that very same day, the residents of the farmlands of Esmere Grange along with the neighbors over at Hampden Hall, the surrounding tenant farmers, and those who lived in and near the village, had heard of the letter's contents:

"My brother, the commanding officer of the log fort on Point Henry in Kingston, Canada, due to his fondness for your relative, Miss Smythe, has arranged for her to stay at my home upon her arrival in London." At this point in her reading of the letter, Lady Esmere informed her husband, in loud emotional strains, "The general's sister is none other than *the* Lady Francesca Rowe."

As no real answer could be given for such a statement, she continued reading, aloud this time: "Miss Smythe has made the journey from Canada in good health and will be arriving in Leaside on Friday next. The short delay in London was necessary, as her servant had experienced great distress and illness due to the crossing."

The private message delivered into Titus Evan Rhodes's hands was longer than the other missive. Shocked that he, too, had received a letter concerning his neighbor's niece, Titus unfolded it in a serious and wary mood. Ever since he had arrived in the small community of Leaside, near Torquay, as the ten-year-old stepson of the old earl of Hampden, Francesca had claimed him as her special friend. But she never wrote to him unless she required a favor.

On his return from Spain and Portugal, he had relied heavily upon her for companionship. He'd thought nothing of asking her for aid, as he was the one who had introduced Rowe to her, hoping at the time that they would suit each other. He'd even stood up with Rowe at the wedding.

The thought of rushing home to Leaside where he would merely be the older, and wounded, half-brother of Jaimie Artemis Clennon, the new Earl of

Hampden, had at first seemed a monumental task. At Francesca's elegant London residence, her household staff had nursed him into sheer boredom and he had returned home, welcoming the task of right-hand man to the earl. Jaimie considered the running of vast farmlands a chore too routine for such a gentleman as himself.

> Titus, my good friend,
>
> See to it that Madeline Smythe is not eaten alive by that specious aunt of hers. You know of whom I speak. Madeline and I have shopped everyday since her voyage and have accomplished a miracle, as it is almost impossible to acquire a wardrobe so quickly. I could not in good conscience send her to Leaside without proper attire.
>
> It is my opinion that this darling daughter of Hilda's is a sensitive young woman of gentle nature and superior intellect, and shall make your dear little brother, the earl, a loyal wife.
>
> Yes, the news of the betrothal was in last Tuesday's mail. She should marry off her own daughter n'est-ce pas?
>
> My regards to the family,
>
> Francesca Rowe

Titus chuckled. He knew well of whom she spoke. Almira Esmere, Bradford's wife, the one behind the betrothal, he'd wager on it. He understood the purpose of Francesca's letter. The Canadian niece must be a rustic, possibly not a looker, and this was Francesca's way of warning him to see she was greeted with warm affection. All who knew Lady Esmere were aware of her biting tongue where young ladies were concerned. The thirty-three-year-old aunt did not care to see herself as a seasoned matron and dressed her own daughter as a schoolgirl instead of the young lady she obviously was. One had to but view the daughter's ample bosom to guess her age.

Almira generally flirted with every male visitor, and all but Titus flirted back. Because Titus ignored her, she despised him, and Titus mistrusted her.

His friend, Francesca Rowe, had long held a grudge against Almira for marrying Bradford, the man she claimed as her own childhood sweetheart.

Now at last it was Friday and all were assembled to greet the young woman who could, with her sizable inheritance from her maternal grandparent, save Hampden Hall.

Titus was the last to arrive on this momentous occasion. Even as the butler took his hat and cane, he heard the squeaking and thumping of the Rowe carriage as it scrunched to a halt. He hesitated but slightly, then strolled on through the door. Better to join the others and be presented with them than to wait here for her in the corridor. Time enough later to take the girl under his wing.

Titus had not been in the massive drawing room since his Eton years when he and Bradford had romped about freely. How the sunlight managed to slant through the shrouded windows with their heavy curtains of dark red velvet was a mystery indeed. The bulbous and lacquered oddments of furniture flanking the walls did not add cheeriness either.

In contrast to the overlarge furnishings, the majority of the room's occupants were so thin as to resemble beanpoles. All but Della Esmere. Her lovely face was as radiant as ever, but her schoolgirl frock could not hide the voluptuous body beneath. She and Jaimie had been sweethearts since the cradle. They consistently visited back and forth between the two houses. Titus believed Jaimie truly cared for her. As any young man did, Jaimie fell regularly in love with beauties, but Della was his constant. It had always been so.

Titus bowed and uttered his polite greetings just minutes before the footman flung the door wide and the butler announced, "Miss Madeline Rose Smythe."

Bradford Esmere advanced to greet his sister's daughter with outstretched hands. Bradford was a good man. A pity he'd married such a harpy.

2

Had Madeline known her great-grandfather had died last summer, she would never have left Canada. Even Lady Rowe, when she had imparted the news of his passing in his sleep, was shocked that Madeline hadn't heard, that no one at Esmere Grange had bothered to write and inform her.

Madeline stood for a moment just inside the drawing room of her mother's childhood home, confident, yet wary. The room was a particularly large chamber but ugly in the extreme. The gray-and-white marble fireplace stood on the west wall, just as Mama had described it, but where were the sofas and chairs upholstered in pale blue velvet? And the ivory brocade on the walls? This could not be her mother's favorite room.

The thick drapes at the tall windows admitted very little light. If it were not for the exquisite cut-glass chandelier illuminating the gray corners, Madeline would not have noticed the dark-eyed gentleman standing apart from the others. He had been staring at her ever since she stepped across the threshold. For that matter, they all had.

She wasn't sure what she had expected but surely not such a welcome as this.

A servant appeared at the door with a tea tray and Madeline's stomach rumbled. She hoped she would not be expected to engage in long and boring conversations before sampling some of the little triangular sandwiches.

Outdoors the sun had almost set and in Kingston, her friends would long since have finished a hearty meal after a busy day. With that thought of home, Madeline was struck with her first bout of real nostalgia. How she wished this English homecoming could have been with her dear mama and papa beside her.

The smiling gentleman approaching her was clearly Mama's brother. He had her mother's pale skin and wavy, honey-colored hair. "Ah, my dear niece, here you are at last. I am your Uncle Bradford. I hope you are well after your long journey?"

"Yes, thank you. I'm most pleased to meet you." She dipped a small curtsy. Her mother had schooled her in every courtesy expected of a young lady; how and when to speak, smile, eat, walk, sit, stand, and most important, when to keep quiet.

Lady Esmere stepped forward and acknowledged her husband's introduction. Madeline assessed the pretty, empty face and marveled at how young she appeared, for Mama had told her Aunt Almira was only three years younger than Uncle Bradford.

Next came their daughter, Della, dressed in a white muslin gown cut too high in the neck for such a bosomy female. She had beautiful skin, black hair, violet eyes, and was exceptionally pretty, a plump replica of her slim mother.

Then Uncle Bradford presented the young gentleman hovering behind them as Jaimie, Lord Hampden. "Our closest neighbor," he added with emphasis.

This was Jaimie Clennon, the Earl of Hampden, that Francesca Rowe had spoken of.

The earl carried her hand to his lips, retaining his hold a shade longer than politeness demanded. He behaved as though something momentous was expected of him. "I trust your trip was uneventful?"

He was tall with a ruddy complexion, or else his cheeks flushed so because he was as uncomfortable as she. As thin as a fence rail, his form bore the athletic look of hard strength. His long face had the boyish features of the Fort Henry guardsmen whom she'd never see again, and Madeline's heart went out to him.

"On the contrary, there were *so* many new sights." Madeline's smile, though pleasant, held a certain reserve, not from the normal apprehension of meeting strange relatives in a new land, but from the certainty that Francesca's forecast of the future could actually happen.

At last the dark man lounging by the windows roused himself, and Uncle Bradford introduced him as the earl's brother, "Captain Titus Evan Rhodes, our neighborhood's own war hero, home after six years in Portugal and Spain, wounded at Torres Vedras."

The captain's manner intrigued Madeline. If he was not a pirate or a gypsy, then certainly a rogue. Indeed, he had the look of a battle-surviving officer. A medium tall man, he was thickly built with broad shoulders, his dark hair combed back. He had more of an aristocratic face than did his brother, and Madeline assumed there must be a mixture of parents; perhaps the reason the younger brother bore the title of earl rather than this competent-looking warrior with the fathomless black eyes.

"Very pleased to make your acquaintance, my lady." The captain bowed and stood there, patiently awaiting her response.

His stillness unnerved her. *My lady.* There it was. Mama had warned her, as had Francesca. "I am Miss Smythe, and very glad for this warm welcome."

Miss Smythe indeed. Titus checked his reaction to the liltingly accented voice. He knew without doubt that Bradford and Almira Esmere had no notion of the forces they might unleash with the proposed betrothal between Miss Smythe and brother Jaimie. Here was no Della whom Almira could manipulate at will. This young lady was nobody's fool. Even he had expected a rustic provincial, but she was not one whit discomposed as the household had assumed she would be. They should have expected no less. She came from the same stock, after all.

Francesca has indeed been busy. Miss Smythe's pearl-gray traveling outfit reflected the precise elegance for a journey to a family country estate. Her hair was the rich color of smooth honey, her mouth wide and generous. She looked like someone full of good spirits, someone to laugh with and give comfort, but she was far from invulnerable. One unguarded moment had given him a glimpse of her green eyes, and there, merged with a wild energy, he detected uncertainty and a tired sadness. Quickly, he brought forth a nearby chair.

"Thank you. I fear I am quite weary." She loosened the ribbons of her bonnet and sank gratefully onto the chair, gracing him with a stunning smile.

On your toes, chap. For the first time since his return to England, Titus felt truly alive.

At dinner Madeline was surprised that a young and impoverished friend of the earl's, a Mr. Nicholas Wardton, escorted Della into the dining room. Captain Rhodes, directed to Aunt Almira's left, was given a higher position of protocol than the daughter of the house, as Della sat nearest the center.

Della, now in a horrid peach gown, adorned with far too many tucks and frills, sat stabbing at her serving of flaky turbot, pinpointing a resentful stare at Madeline. And rightfully so, Madeline thought, as she, a Canadian relative, had seemingly usurped her place in the household.

At about the ninth course—Madeline had lost count after the sixth or seventh—Uncle Bradford rose from his place at the head of the table. All conversation ceased with his loud harrumphing. He smiled benignly at Madeline and declared, "In a month's time the betrothal of our niece, dear Hilda's daughter, to our good neighbor, Lord Hampden, could be celebrated. All that is needed, dear niece, is for you to give your nod."

Good heavens, the man is serious. Madeline, astonished by his unexpected announcement, glanced for a moment at the earl, then at Della Esmere. Her cousin breathed a gasp, soft yet audible, and Madeline, thankful it had reached her ears, sat stunned. She watched the look on Della's face whip like a shot from one of genuine adoration for the earl to urgent alarm.

Why should her uncle and aunt wish to match her with Lord Hampden when their own daughter seemed the perfect choice?

Francesca Rowe had tried to warn her, but at the time she'd thought nothing of it. "The circumstances," Francesca had related, "are rooted twenty years since. Your mother, the first grandchild, had accepted her grandfather's plan to wed the Earl of Hampden." That would have been Jaimie's father, now deceased. "But once Hilda saw the likes of Colonel Randall Smythe, once he held her in his arms . . ."

Madeline knew her uncle, whose title was derived from the family name, owned vast lands. The neighboring earl had twice as much property, with every last farm encumbered. Which meant Jaimie, the new earl, must make an advantageous match.

Her relatives were proposing that she marry a near penniless earl whom she'd never met until now.

Madeline sensed everyone at the table stiffen. She looked at Uncle Bradford's slim fingers tapping her wrist and realized the assembled company expected her to give an answer. "In one month's time?" she asked, hating the way her voice sounded unsure and as doubtful as the perplexed look on the earl's face. She must be diplomatic with her reply. No need to hurt him unnecessarily. She doubted if he had ever been spurned before. "I am not unlike any other in that I care about the formalities of courtship as much as the next lady. Perhaps during this month, the earl and I might scrape an acquaintance with each other. We could go for rides, walks, dance together. Could we not?" She paused, observing the reactions of the main players in this farce. "Then Lord Hampden," she smiled at Jaimie to give him confidence, if not reassurance, "will wish to consider his future."

"Bravo!" Nicholas Wardton shouted from the end of the table. Amid the clapping and congratulatory comments, Madeline felt sure she was the only one who observed Della Esmere slip silently from the room.

Captain Rhodes chuckled and thought how he was enjoying himself after all. If Francesca could see her prodigy now. Miss Smythe is more like to eat Almira Esmere than the other way round. He leaned back in his chair and soaked up the carnival atmosphere. This was better than Drury Lane.

Early the next morning, Madeline heard voices outside her bedroom window. Still stiff and sluggish from yesterday's carriage ride, she drew back the drapes and peered out. Lord Hampden and Della stood in the courtyard, so preoccupied with each other they did not even hear her lift the latch on the window frame. It was only then that Madeline realized how splendid Della looked in her riding dress, the jacket fitting her form to perfection. She is such a beauty, she thought.

She had intended to call to the couple when she heard Lord Hampden say, "This changes nothing, Della. It is only your pride speaking. You know we'll always be friends, and someday you will fall in love, truly."

Madeline ducked behind the chintz drapes, clanking the curtain rings. Dear heavens, what a thing to say to a girl who loves him. What is he thinking?

Then she heard Della accuse, "You have already proposed to me, more than once I might add."

The earl chuckled. "We were mere children, Della girl."

She could not hear Della's reply, but whatever it was, she definitely uttered it in anger. A wild scramble of horse's hooves clattered on the tiled courtyard. Madeline dared peek again and saw Della galloping off in the distance at a reckless speed. She'd left the earl slicing the hedge with his riding crop.

What to do? Facing the uncertainties of life in Kingston as an unmarried woman would have been a welcome alternative compared to causing such upheaval in another's life. If Jaimie had already proposed to her cousin, if there was a prearranged alliance between Jaimie and Della, then she might

find a way out of this mess without giving the earl a
flat refusal.

Madeline had had many opportunities for
romance, living as she had in the midst of such
handsome, and lonely, soldiers in Kingston. Some
she had considered more seriously than others, but
she categorized them all as friendly relationships.
The garrison duty at Fort Henry grew extremely
tedious at times, and the good general and his wife,
along with all his married officers and their
spouses, kept up a continuous social schedule,
mainly for the benefit of the guardsmen.

Social graces were not nonexistent in Kingston
but were more lax than the rigid rules of the English
aristocracy. Aside from barn raisings and picnics,
there were few social happenings, so most inhabitants of the town and surrounding farms and forests
flocked to the regularly held assemblies. Only during
battle times did the gaity completely cease.

Madeline had been raised as any young English
girl of quality would have been had her parents
remained in England after her birth. And her
mother's Irish maid had personally trained Esther.

Madeline's outspokenness and impulsive nature
were a result of her personality and her exposure to
the settlers of the Province; the lowliest servant in
England could, after immigrating to Canada, own
vast lands if he could perform the back-breaking
labor needed to keep it. She thought it wonderful
they did not have to answer to an estate manager,
or a landlord, as they would have in England.

Even in Kingston life had been rustic, and
Madeline had helped her mother assist at both

births and deaths. They had followed to the letter the pioneer families' directions for laying out the dead. Cooking and sewing were second nature to Madeline. When her own mother died, she had taken on the chores, along with the officers' wives, of providing food and clothing for orphaned children and of letter writing for the guardsmen. As an unattached female, though forbidden to care for the wounded men, she had measured, cut, and rolled bandages for hours at a time.

Tranforming Della into a bride the earl could not resist did not seem an enormous task at all.

Captain Titus Evan Rhodes's residence stood at the edge of the village. Living alone in his modest home suited him; he had slept too often in army encampments to care whether he wallowed in immaculate splendor as did Jaimie.

It was a rainy, cold, dismal day and his leg ached like hell. He built his own fire in the grate and settled back in his brown leather chair and was having a glass of wine when Sheridan answered the door knocker.

"Your brother, the earl," Sheridan announced as he backed from the study.

Titus flung out his hand, indicating that Jaimie should sit. Jaimie obliged, blabbing full tilt of the approaching Esmere's evening party. "There is to be dancing after dinner, Titus. You *are* going?"

"Wild horses couldn't drag me." When the wound in his leg pained him terribly, dancing was out. Mere speech was out.

"Titus, I need you to be there! Della is cutting up something dreadful about this betrothal thing—"

"Don't expect me to keep your ladies entertained," Titus said emphatically. He gave a grim chuckle. "I expect a show indeed while Miss Smythe keeps you in line. Damn shock for the Esmeres last evening when she didn't grovel at the mention of marriage to an earl. The woman has a mind of her own."

"The woman has a title. She's Lady Madeline."

Titus ignored that. *We'll see.* It was no wonder he had not entered into matrimony; it wasn't as though he had not had the whole neighborhood of available ladies pushed at him at some time or another. Like Jaimie, Titus found most of the well-brought-up ladies roundabout dead bores, but Miss Smythe. Now here was a challenge indeed.

"Do you good to go round more. Stay cooped up here too much."

Compared to the younger set Jaimie ran with, and their frustrations concerning women, Titus felt nothing but gratitude for his quiet existence. In the past, he'd had no problem finding women to share his life, or his bed.

He shuddered to think what would have happened to him if it hadn't been for Sheridan, his batman. He could not have left the military without his stiff and proper orderly.

And Francesca. On his return to London, he'd accepted her offer of a room in her home with her servants caring for him during his early recuperation from his wound. Those two were true friends and their devotion and loyalty were extraordinary.

Jaimie, determined as usual, continued his cursed persuading, droning on and on.

"Hell," Titus muttered through gritted teeth. No point in arguing with him. If Jaimie didn't get his way, he would simply petition their mother with a request that she speak to his demented brother.

Titus decided he would go to the Esmere's evening party. He didn't want their mother's visit to Bath disturbed. Besides which, he owed Francesca a favor.

Madeline told Esther her plan and insisted they skip breakfast and hop right to it. Munching apples Esther had swiped from the kitchen, they paced in the stable yard, awaiting Della's return. There was not a minute to lose.

As soon as Della dismounted, Madeline seized her by the elbow, directing her toward the house, out of earshot and away from the groom slanting a curious look after them. Tossing her apple core, Madeline asked, "We are to have dancing after dinner tonight, correct? Neighbors from the village and the surrounding countryside are invited?"

Della pulled her arm away. "You requested dancing, did you not? My mother has engaged musicians." Her tone was cold, hostile even.

"Yes, but I'm just a colonial woman and have no notion of polite society."

Here, Esther stared at Madeline, her eyebrows raised.

Della tucked her riding crop under her arm. "What do you want of me?"

"Oh, please, you must help me. I'm so nervous about the party tonight. Could you show me how to go on?" Madeline pleaded in her most urgent voice.

At this, Esther's face blazed. "Well, I never!" She swiveled round, stuffed her hands under her stiff pinafore, and stomped into the house through the kitchen door.

"Why should I help you? You have everything I want."

Madeline's stomach lurched. This was indeed harder than she had anticipated. Better to be truthful. "Now listen, I have no intention of marrying your sweetheart. I'll choose my own husband when and if I find him. No, don't interrupt. There's a way out of this coil."

The change in Della's attitude after Madeline confessed she had no designs on the earl was, to say the least, sunny.

They retired to Della's suite of rooms where Esther waited. Madeline circled Della, surveying her and muttering to herself. Her appearance cannot be the reason they weren't matching her with the earl. She was breathtakingly beautiful from the neck up, just a bit plump. "You know, there is only one acquaintance of mine back in Kingston who is even a wee bit—uh, and she does no work whatsoever. Sits around eating sweetmeats, puddings, pies. She never dances at the assemblies." A sudden idea slipped into focus. She faced Della. "Do you ride every day?"

"No. I was used to meet Jaimie on Saturday and Sunday mornings for a go round the countryside, but I vow I'll not meet him again."

"Make no vows yet, please." If she could manage riding and long walks with Della every day, maybe—

"Esther, do you think we can let out the seams of that new dark satin gown Lady Rowe packed for me? The midnight blue with the pearl buttons?" The color would match Della's violet eyes, and the clean, simple lines should have the same effect as the elegant riding outfit. Madeline could picture Della wearing it to dinner, and she was determined to seat her beside the earl, no matter what.

Something had to be done with that jumbled and curly mass of black hair. Cut it, of course, but only a trim. "Esther, call for Della's maid. You must teach her a thing or two about dressing hair."

After the dark curls were cut and swept away, Della persuaded them to wait for the seamstress. She vowed the elderly woman would be devastated if she was not allowed in on this great secret project.

Madeline knew it was no secret and hadn't been since Della's little maid, Pixie, had been summoned. Not since the maids served a nuncheon on a tray and had been allowed to eat in the same room. She smiled at Della standing patiently in the middle of the determined women. She took it very well indeed, the draping, puffing, pinning, and occasional pricking. She even seemed to enjoy the attention.

When the altered dress was finished, the four women gushed effusively over their handiwork. "What an exorbitant change," Della declared, as she primped before the long pier glass.

Good heavens, Madeline thought. If Della set foot on Canadian soil, she would be a sought-after beauty with swarms of suitors. The single guardsmen and male settlers, yearning for women with pretty faces and strong constitutions, would gobble her up in no time. Managing alone was rare in the wilds, and women were treated as coveted creatures.

Della had a straight, proud posture, a way of holding her head. What a general she would make, Madeline thought, or better yet, a countess. She was a favorite of the servants, too. When she yanked the bellcord in her suite, any number came running.

But the biggest shock for Madeline came late in the afternoon when Pixie announced it was time for her to help set out tea over at Hampden Hall, and taking her leave, off she went.

Madeline turned to Della. "You mean . . . she is under the earl's employ?"

"Oh, yes. My mother says I don't need an abigail just yet. Better to wait until I am older. Pixie and I have been friends since we were babies. She rides over daily with the eggman."

Madeline and Esther exchanged perplexed looks, and Della added, "Jaimie's mother allows it."

"Why wasn't she invited to the dinner on Friday evening?" Madeline asked, trying for an unconcerned tone. "Jaimie's mother?"

"Oh, she is somewhat sickly and is vacationing in Bath, though the captain says once she removes to the Dower House he thinks she'll be fine again. She would have moved there straightaway, but it is a draughty and uncomfortable mess. The roof leaks and every room is in need of paint. The captain is transforming the house for her, since the Hampden estate has no money to spare."

"Why would she have moved there? The Hall is her home, is it not? I mean, she is Jaimie's mother, and he is unmarried."

"She has always disliked the Hall. Can't abide the Gothic architecture."

"And you? Do you hate it?"

"Oh, no. I love the gargoyles, the finials, and the wooded park. My nanny owned I could run loose there and never be lost. I know every corner."

There it was again, the mystery of why not ally Della and the earl? Surely their great-grandmother's portion would be divided between the two of them. Both she and Della were her descendants.

3

"*Della!*" *Aunt Almira's voice* shrieked up the stairwell. "Where did you find such a dress?"

Madeline peeked over the bannister. Her aunt stood below, staring at Della as though she had seen a ghost.

The whole day's project in Della's bedchamber had gone on without Aunt Almira's knowledge. It's her own fault, thought Madeline. If she hadn't ignored Della for so long . . . And Uncle Bradford was no better. He rode out early, probably with a bailiff, and there simply was no one else to monitor Della's activities.

Madeline reached the bottom of the stairs first and stepped in front of Della. "The dress was mine, Aunt Almira, but doesn't it suit Della? I have an abundance of gowns, and this one was too utterly perfect for Della to waste on me. With my coloring, it wouldn't do. Doesn't she look lovely?"

Madeline took in once more the midnight blue gown that matched Della's sparkling eyes. Francesca had insisted she purchase the satiny garment, saying that young ladies needed color to compliment their faces instead of forever dressing in pale tints and chaste white. She had declared it a waste of youthful beauty to dress only mature ladies in the more fashionable hues. Indeed, Della looked smart in the elegantly tailored skirt over petticoats trimmed with satin ribbons of the same shade.

Aunt Almira turned a wrathful face toward Madeline, but Uncle Bradford bowed before them and kissed Della on the forehead. "You are beautiful, darling girl."

Madeline smiled, delighted with his reaction toward his daughter, and Della, wide-eyed and laughing at her father's comment, blushed and ignored her mother's sputterings.

Madeline caught sight of her image alongside Della's in the hall mirror and thought they looked like any two young ladies ready for an entertaining evening, her own jade gown complimenting the dark midnight blue of Della's. Satisfied that the day's work had indeed been worth the effort, she tucked one of her jeweled combs more firmly into place, then tugged at the fashionable long gloves covering her arms. She wished the dinner guests would hurry and arrive before Aunt Almira could say more and ruin the mood. She'd taken very little from the lunch tray and was famished.

"Della, go and change immediately," Aunt Almira commanded through thin lips.

"No, I—"

They all heard the door knocker at the same time. *Just in the nick,* Madeline thought. Probably Della would not have consented to the bizarre day's project if not for the cavalier way Jaimie had treated her. Telling her it was only her wounded pride! He had no idea. A woman scorned and all that; she shuddered to think what might lie in store for the earl. Yes, Della could handle him well enough.

And in he walked, accompanied by his brother, Captain Rhodes, the black-eyed pirate-hero of Leaside.

Madeline stared at the magnificent figure of the captain, his posture maddeningly self-assured, his face as bland as Mama had told her a fashionable Englishman, or lady, could manage at any hour. The unwritten rule was that ladies and gentlemen never allowed their emotions to show on their faces. She needn't have bothered hiding her reaction, for he was gaping at her. But no, not at her. She sighed, realizing he and the earl had stared for a moment at Della. So, it was working. What they needed next was for the men of the community to see Della in a different light. If the captain was affected, the others should be also, and in particular, Jaimie.

The earl greeted her warmly, but she barely acknowledged him, busy as she was observing the captain, the way he moved with long fluid strides, on occasion favoring his right leg. His rakish grin and the confidence shining in his eyes were proof he knew she admired him. Laughing at herself, she smiled as he bowed and kissed her hand. She had never been able to hide her feelings and saw no reason to change now.

After dinner hired musicians fiddled and scraped out some tunes. Jaimie opened the dancing with Madeline, and Captain Rhodes squired Della. For the next set, Mr. Wardton met them at the edge of the room and bowed to Madeline, while the captain ordered Jaimie dance with Della. Off Jaimie went, glaring over his shoulder at his brother.

The third dance was a waltz and Della had to refuse Mr. Wardton's request. Aunt Almira forbid her, saying, "Della is much too young." So Mr. Wardton took a seat beside Della, raising Madeline's opinion of him several notches.

The captain had meandered his way across the room with Uncle Bradford and Aunt Almira. Madeline's first thought was to join Della and her new admirer, but just as she took a step she saw the captain cross the room in a flash, closing in on her. She stood her ground and he was beside her in moments. She met his gaze, noting the eyes she had thought black were a deep rich brown. His skin was olive, his chin and right cheek ravaged with tiny nicks and scars. He stepped closer and Madeline inhaled the warm brush of port and the familiar scent of polished military boots.

"What a transformation has taken place," he said in a low voice. "Did some good witch weave her spell here today?"

Madeline's mouth went suddenly dry. "Whatever do you mean?"

"You know very well. Della. She looks more the thing than I can ever remember."

"She's a goddess, isn't she?"

"I wouldn't go that far, but yes, she is lovely, as we all know." He moved even closer. "You had a hand in this."

She couldn't deny it. "I find her mother's treatment of her appalling, but apparently Della is accustomed to it."

The captain nodded and whispered, "Lady Esmere's belief in her own beauty has not blinded her to Della's splendid appeal. I think she is reluctant to appear beside her daughter in the London drawing rooms. She is busy coaxing Bradford to purchase a town house for the season." His smile hinted at mockery.

Relieved that here was someone who thought as she did, Madeline told him a little of her background, the long way round. Of how her mother's Irish maid had trained Esther, her present abigail. And how Madeline, in short skirts, witnessed the extensive training and learned the lessons well herself. "My mother took pains to see I knew how to go on. That is perhaps one of the reasons I feel so at ease here." At ease, but not truly at home. "And why I attempted to help Della. She seemed neglected—" Conscious of her rude rambling, she said, "I did not mean to speak ill of your friends, and my relatives, the Esmeres."

"Think nothing of it. I agree with you. Up until your arrival, Della was indeed ignored, but not from a lack of love. Has Lady Esmere any comments concerning her daughter tonight?"

"Yes," was all Madeline could say without bursting into laughter. She and the captain turned their gazes on Almira, who greeted her guests with thin, determined lips.

In his hoarse, military growl, Captain Rhodes said, "What lies ahead for our Della, eh? If Bradford would only exert some influence in her regard, but he truly considers her still his little girl."

"He is not blind certainly."

He looked at her, amusement in his eyes.

She laughed; she couldn't help herself. And for the first time she felt she might belong here after all.

"Will you dance?" the captain asked after a quiet moment.

Madeline nodded, and he took her elbow, guiding her onto the dance floor. Face-to-face, body to body, the aura of the man was more rattling than when she had first noticed him from a safe distance across the room. She felt lightheaded in his presence, in his arms.

Reining in her wild thoughts, Madeline admonished herself to be alert with him at all times. She doubted she could put anything over on him, but instinctively she trusted the man. Perhaps because she had grown up around his sort. He walked, talked, and barked orders like the officers at Fort Henry.

In a low voice she said, "My mother told me that Great-Grandfather and the old Earl of Hampden had always wished to join the two estates?"

"True. The land has passed from generation to generation, and my stepfather believed if the two properties united, it would always be so."

"Is it imperative that the earl wed at this time? He seems . . . quite young."

"One and twenty is young, indeed," the captain replied. "He must marry a woman of wealth."

"I expect you're right."

"He would then have the blunt for his horses, the gaming tables, and his other—private pursuits."

Madeline knew better than to ask what pursuits, but she was surprised the captain had not tried to forestall the discussion of his brother's affairs.

"Then there's Lady Esmere's desires to consider—her plans to enter London society after you and Jaimie are wed. When the Hampden accounts are settled. Speaking of the accounts, besides the house servants who must be paid each month, there are the bailiffs, game wardens, gardeners, and the occasional help from the village."

Madeline's appalled reaction must have been evident, for he finished with:

"I am that glad Jaimie is the peer, and not me. Hell of a task."

In the music room, rows of chairs had been set up by the Palladian windows where Jaimie stood frantically waving for the captain, and Della sat conversing in a loud voice with Mr. Wardton.

Frowning, Captain Rhodes steered Madeline in their direction.

The evening was going along well. Della had attracted much attention. It was evident she was happier and that made her seem even prettier.

Straightaway, Madeline requested lemonade. The gentlemen departed and she praised Della's behavior. "Flirting with Mr. Wardton," she said.

"What a smart idea. When Jaimie notices the others have an interest in you, he'll be after you right enough. Gentlemen love chasing after the ladies."

Della turned her pert nose to Madeline. "Jaimie wants to stand up with only you."

Madeline looked at her searchingly. "We only had the one, and it was a duty dance."

"Hah! I've never seen a duty look so much like a pleasure before."

Later in the evening, Madeline noticed that Jaimie wore a piqued expression when Della stood up with any of the young gentlemen. When she had two dances with Mr. Wardton, Jaimie looked positively irritable.

Madeline seized the earl for the next waltz and filled his ears full of chatter about what a fitting couple they looked, "Della and Mr. Wardton," she said, "quite a couple."

"Hmmm," Jaimie said noncommittally.

"So handsome together with his blond mustache and her dark curls."

"You are a beauty, you know."

She managed a weak smile.

"And it's working out perfectly."

"What do you mean?"

"I never imagined we would hit it off so well, so soon," he replied, his eyebrows wiggling suggestively.

"Indeed?" she croaked.

"I've admired you from the moment you stepped into my life, and when you floated into my arms just now as though you couldn't wait to have me hold you—"

"We are merely waltzing." *The man is insane!*

"Yes, what an exquisite suggestion of yours, my dear. That we have a courtship. Romantic, isn't it? Not at all what I expected of an arranged marriage. Everyone is happy for us."

Madeline was in shock. Sure enough, the faces swimming around the room smiled and nodded approval. How could she have bungled things so horribly?

"Tomorrow morning we will go for a ride. Just the two of us. Promise you'll meet me in the courtyard."

She didn't answer. She couldn't.

"If you don't, I shall throw pebbles at your window," he coaxed.

In Madeline's mind burned the image of Della's confrontation with Jaimie under her bedroom window. She groaned and instantly regretted it, for he took it as a sign of rapturous expectation.

"My dear!" he exclaimed.

The music crashed to a stop. They were near the archway to the corridor and Madeline wanted nothing more than to sneak through it and disappear, but wisdom prevailed. She had started this farce and must stick to the plan.

As soon as the last guests took their leave, Aunt Almira cut up at Madeline. "You are an unsettling influence on Della. She has always been a headstrong child, and the foolishness you are feeding her will surely goad her to misbehavior."

Madeline secretly hoped so, wondering what hole Della was hiding in at this very moment. She should be here fighting her own battles. "A woman of eighteen is no longer a child."

"I know what is best for my own daughter," Almira said.

Her aunt's voice held a note of finality that ended further discussion of Della.

"And you, introducing yourself as a miss. Good God, girl, your uncle is a baron. When you are married you will be a countess! You cannot go around calling yourself a *miss*."

"I have always been Miss Smythe."

"Rid yourself of your provincial ways," Almira said emphatically, as she left the room with a swish of her taffeta skirts.

Madeline bristled at her aunt's dismissal. Almira's domineering attitude was just the right prod to convince Madeline that she was heading in the right direction.

But that night she slept fitfully. She had a terrible sense that events were no longer apt to fall into place.

4

Madeline moaned into her pillow. "Stop it, Della, I'm awake." Della had burst into Madeline's bedroom and was shaking her with a vengeance.

"How did you know it was me?"

"No one else slams into a room like you."

"Your betrothed will be expecting you. Hurry now, you wouldn't want to keep him waiting."

"I am not betrothed," Madeline said under her breath.

She stared as Della stamped to the window and yanked the curtains apart. How did Della discover the earl had invited her for a ride? Surely Jaimie would not have told her.

"I daresay there is a sharp wind about and riding would be a dreadful pain in such weather." She gave Della a wavering smile.

"What? Are you backing down?" Della accused from the foot of the carved bedstead.

"Why don't you come?" Madeline offered.

"I wouldn't think of it. Jaimie will wish for privacy with you." She crossed to the door. "I'll just pop out and arrange a mount for you."

Esther, standing in the doorway with a tray of toast and hot chocolate, gaped at Della as she passed.

"What have you been up to?" She set the tray on the table near the fireplace.

"Don't ask."

Dreading the day, Madeline dressed quickly. She meant to leave before Della had the mount brought around, intending to go on foot toward the Hall so she could meet the earl away from the house. She had no doubt Della would be lurking about at some window or doorway near the courtyard.

"You can't go out without breakfast," Esther said.

"I can't eat," Madeline stammered. She knew meeting the earl was a dreadful mistake, but how could she possibly disentangle herself?

Unsure what to do, what to say, Madeline paused downstairs at the door. Why should she even attempt an explanation? She had not asked for this role.

But she had to go. It was what her parents would have expected of her. As a member of a British army family, her duties had been spelled out. She must help those around her, and not only those least able to help themselves. She must lend moral support, and, she supposed, that was what Jaimie would need just now.

She swallowed, breathed deeply, and hurried down the lane.

✳   ✳   ✳

As he pulled on his riding gloves, Titus checked with Sheridan. The orderly-turned-butler and valet silently opened the door to the study.

His arms wrapped around him, Jaimie snored on the divan by the cold grate, the covers thrown every which way. Titus chuckled. *Good. He'll sleep for several hours yet.* Admonishing Sheridan to keep a close watch, he left the house.

Last night he had finagled Wardton into meeting them at the Green Dragon Inn, then he had assisted Jaimie and Wardton with drinking themselves silly, leaving Wardton on his own for the innkeeper. Jaimie never could hold his liquor, and Titus thought a drunken stupor the best way to keep him from meeting with Miss Smythe.

Pity Della has her mother's dark hair and dainty facial features. What a great solution to the problem here if she could have been blessed with Bradford's hair color, or his hazel eyes. Bradford loved the girl as his own, no uncertainty there, but he'd let slip more than once that he doubted Della was truly his offspring. Years ago, her mother's overfamiliarity with every man she met convinced Bradford that he couldn't trust her.

Once when Titus and Bradford had rushed home on furlough, Bradford had found Almira ensconced in the drawing room, a besotted expression on her face as she served tea to half a dozen gentlemen callers. Whispers around the neighborhood soon convinced him his wife was not sitting idly at home awaiting his presence.

After their return to the unit, Bradford had managed to sell his commission, and he'd been playing watchdog to Almira's flirting ever since. When Della was born, he petitioned his grandmother to cut the newborn from the portion due all female grandchildren. Titus wondered if the elegant old lady had listened to Bradford and his ravings. He knew for a certainty that she claimed Della as her own flesh and blood, whether Bradford did or not.

He came upon Miss Smythe at the bend in the lane connecting the two estates. She was walking swiftly, head and shoulders back, dressed in a riding habit and carrying a matching plumed hat in her hand. She looked splendid as she came forward, her skirt well tailored over polished leather boots. She had poise that belied her years, and with such a young face he thought it impossible she could be four and twenty.

He dismounted, disliking the way his senses stood at attention. A combat veteran, he instinctively set up defenses. If you are to save your brother from this bewitching female, old man, you must first save yourself.

Miss Smythe looked annoyed. "Where is the earl?"

He bowed. "Good day to you, too."

"Good morning. I . . ." She trailed off, apparently deciding she needn't offer an excuse for her lack of manners. She twisted the buckling bands of her hat together.

"The earl had a bit too much to drink after the dancing. He asked me to come in his stead."

She sighed, clearly not pleased. "You purposely kept him away."

"Yes," he answered, maintaining his composure despite his irritation with her for finding him out. "Where is your mount?"

"I came on foot because I had no intention of riding out with him." She ran her fingertips along the brim of the hat. "I merely wanted to . . . talk."

"May I ask what about?"

"Presumptuous of you to ask."

"Did you wake up on the wrong side of the bed this morning?"

She threw him a long look before saying, "I wanted to speak to him about my decision concerning our proposed betrothal."

"You expected to meet him without a groom, or your abigail." He searched her face. "Is that usual for young ladies of Canada?"

Her eyes narrowed. He could see she was incensed at his critical tone. "Actually, no. A guardsman always accompanied me if I traveled far. The general saw to it, for both my maid and myself. Why is it any of your concern?"

He did not offer an answer, recalling Jaimie's comments about her last night at the inn. "A charming girl," he'd said, "if a trifle high-spirited."

If Jaimie only knew.

She added, "Now that I am in this charming country, I do not feel the need for an escort."

"All the more need," he growled. "It is easy for a lady to acquire a loose reputation. Even here in the country." Titus recognized and admired independence in others, but bullheadedness could hinder a person's better judgment. He should know.

What's more, he knew this primitive attraction

he felt surging through his veins could land him in a heap of trouble.

What the hell. With one move he was beside her, so close, with hardly a breath between them. He lifted her into his saddle, mounting behind her.

In a startled voice she asked, "Doesn't a gentleman usually ask a lady if she wishes an escort?"

He nodded curtly as he entwined the reins in his hand while wrapping his arms around her. "Would you be so kind as to accept my assistance?"

"I suppose I have no choice."

Was that amusement he heard in her voice? "We need a private place in which to discuss the situation." Along the lane was a stone boundary wall. He headed the horse straight for it. "Hold tight to that hat, Miss Smythe."

He cleared the wall with ease, having made the jump many times in the past with whatever pony he happened to commandeer.

Miss Smythe's firm hold of his arms loosened and she relaxed against him as they galloped across the broad empty field beyond the wall. He didn't want to mislead her. A warning, that was his intention. She didn't deserve Almira Esmere's manipulations.

Titus slowed the horse to a trot as they came to the wooded park of Hampden Hall. The light scent of her hair was a mixture of lavender and oranges. He inhaled deeply and at once was aware of the soft swell of her breasts under the snowy fabric of her shirt. He could feel his heart pounding against her back. He had known she would be a challenge, but his great mistake was underestimating her appeal.

He reined in the gray stallion beside a stone bench. Dismounting, he raised his arms to help her down when she slid against him, landing on the ground as nimbly as if she rode double every day. This was a new experience for him and one he hoped to repeat.

They could hear the morning birds in the aspens. Thin wisps of fog floated upward, but the sun had barely shown itself above the line of hawthorn bushes beyond the thick and shadowed forest. Mayhap he'd made a mistake bringing her here, but now was not the time to dwell on it.

The bench, moist with dew, glistened in the morning light. "We cannot sit here. Come, we'll walk a ways." He helped her across a dried rillet and up a grassy slope to a clearing edged with thick honeysuckle hedges. She held on to his hand until they reached the path bordering it.

"You don't seem to have much to say," he blurted out, then was sorry for saying it. He had liked the quiet walk beside her. Even though they both wore gloves, he'd felt the warmth of her hand in his.

"I love walking in the woods. Are you fond of honeysuckle?" She smiled and breathed deeply. "The fragrance is heavenly, isn't it?"

He nodded, thinking it wise that he return to the subject at hand.

"Lady Rowe must have warned you of Lady Esmere's plan. Yet you seemed thoroughly surprised when your uncle made the announcement."

"I didn't expect he would mention it on my first night here, but that wasn't why I was surprised. I couldn't help wondering about Della. They are a pair, she and your brother, yet my aunt and uncle don't seem to see it. Or as you say, Aunt Almira refuses to admit that Della is full blown."

"Excellent choice of words."

She laughed and finally put on the much twisted hat, slanting it at an angle. He loved the way she gazed at him from under the brim. The uncertainty in her eyes had disappeared.

"You found me out," she said, "at the dancing party. Della is a challenge, but what an organizer she will be one day. I confess she gives me a purpose, and a reason for my wish to speak with your brother."

"Bored out of your mind are you?"

She laughed again and the gay sound spiraled down his spine.

"Not at all, Captain. And I do apologize for my rudeness when we first met this morning. I was, uh, awakened rather abruptly."

"Ah, so I was correct."

"The wrong side of the bed? My worst fault is my grumpy disposition when I don't sleep well."

"Perhaps you have not adjusted to your new home, or to our customs that must seem peculiar to you, and relatives you've never before met?"

She smiled. "Something similar, yes."

He wondered if she realized that she owed Lady Esmere's reception to the general in Canada who had the good sense to send her first to Francesca Rowe. Almira Esmere held great awe for Francesca's exalted position in London society and would do nothing to mar her own reputation in that light.

"Do not feel that you must obey Lady Esmere's every command," he said.

"I quite agree. She was upset with Della and her new clothes, but what angered her the most was my interference."

They turned back toward the wooded park, and Titus took her elbow, content to walk with her in silence. She had a way of charming him into believing that she thought being with him was a great adventure. He felt a rush of warmth at the way she threw coquettish glances at him. Was he a fool to think her attracted to him?

At the end of the path he halted and asked softly, "Have you decided?"

"About what?"

"Will you wed him?"

"Why is there a question in your mind?"

"You do not behave toward me as though you are contemplating marriage with another."

Della was waiting at the courtyard door when the captain delivered Madeline safely home.

"Where is Jaimie?" she demanded. "What happened? Why didn't you take out Blackie?"

"One question at a time, Della, please."

The younger woman swept past her, barring passage up the stairway. "Where is he?"

"He didn't show. The captain took his place."

Della's eyes were wide with curiosity. "He didn't?"

Determined not to reveal that the earl was too sapped to mount a horse, she said, "Obviously an early morning ride with me was not enticement enough to drag him from his bed."

Satisfied that Della's irritated expression had turned to a pleased one, Madeline added, "I need a nap." She ran up the stairs and slammed her bedroom door after her, not caring about her rudeness. She had never in her life been so unsettled as she had since arriving at Leaside and meeting this crazy tribe of English. Especially a certain roguish captain.

That afternoon, Lord Hampden sat facing Madeline in the drawing room, apologizing for not meeting her.

"It is quite all right, thank you very much, but an apology is not necessary. I had an enjoyable walk in the park with your brother, the captain."

Lord Hampden's face paled, then reddened. "The captain."

Madeline nodded. "He met me in your stead."

"It has been his habit in the past to take the reins where I have been lax."

"I quite understand. It must be a pain to always have someone about who does the pretty. Does he often remind you of your duties?"

His face grew redder, if possible. "On the contrary. I could not have been blessed with a finer brother."

At first he had appeared angry with Captain Rhodes, now he was singing his praises. She would never understand men. "Of course. I meant nothing untoward. Could the wound my uncle mentioned . . . Captain Rhodes seems to favor his right leg."

"With his colonel he led his squadron across enemy territory—a night attack, mind you—with gross fighting in the trenches. Colonel March was killed, but Titus advanced to capture the position." He paused, staring at the carpet. There was not a sound in the room. "Blames himself for his colonel's death. It is not true. Those things happen in battle.

"His grace, Wellington, you know, called him up for Brussels, but Titus's leg wound enabled him to sell out. Surprised the hell out of all of us, let me tell you. Oh, sorry about the language."

"Think nothing of it."

"Good thing, his selling out. Else he would most definitely have been at Waterloo."

Madeline nodded. "By the time I arrived in London at Lady Rowe's, it was June, two months spent traveling, yet the time passed quickly, and everywhere people spoke gravely of Bonaparte. The stories were both fascinating and abhorrent. At home I was so engrossed with the aftermath of our war with North America that I didn't give a thought to other matters."

Madeline's first impression of Lord Hampden had been that he seemed a rich and spoiled son of a powerful man. One of the type so used to receiving his own way he simply did not understand the word *no*. He had seemed such a child she had wondered why Della was in love with him. But she could see now there was more man here, more character, than she had previously witnessed.

She said, "Lady Rowe had firsthand news in London. Many of her friends returned to town before the battle took place. When I left she still had not heard from all the ladies who chose to stay in Brussels with their husbands."

The earl's gaze held hers. "I expect I would have been there if my father were still alive. As it is, I have the responsibility of remaining behind. The family estates, you know."

Titus sat at the Green Dragon nursing a mug of ale and wolfing down huge bites of a meat pie. He knew from his travels in the army not to ask the source of the meat. He merely swallowed and gulped it down with the locally brewed ale.

He and Bradford had just returned from London where Titus had signed his freedom away. For the time being, anyway.

Before his death, the old earl, Titus's stepfather, had made Titus trustee and guardian over Jaimie's inheritance, with Bradford temporary guardian until Titus should return from active duty. When Jaimie reached the age of five and twenty, he would be in sole control. In the meantime, Jaimie received an allowance for his own personal entertainments. Since the old earl's death, Bradford had been in charge of doling out salaries for the help, but he had not made much headway toward the debts. He wondered if Almira had had her hand in the till. *No, impossible.* Titus had flatly refused the position of guardianship until he discovered Almira's plot to marry off her niece to Jaimie. Then, after his meeting with Miss Smythe, he had decided he must step in.

Bradford was calling for more ale when Jaimie

stormed into the private parlor, accusing Titus of treason, or worse.

"And what's this Sheridan tells me about a trip to London?" Jaimie swore, glancing at Bradford. "You haven't gone and taken the reins? You've accepted the trusteeship! I'll be damned. What else am I to learn from my neighbors and their servants?"

"Neighbors? What are you yelling about?" Titus searched his face suspiciously.

Jaimie placed his hands on the table and leaned forward. "Lady Madeline told me about your little walk in the woods."

Titus responded with exaggerated good humor, despite it rankling that Miss Smythe had told Jaimie about their walk. "You were fast asleep and smelling ghastly."

"My own brother staging a march on me."

"It isn't what you think, yet—" Jaimie's scowling expression reminded Titus of his stepfather, only Jaimie's was gentle compared to the old curmudgeon's. "I couldn't pass up an opportunity for flirtation with a lovely lady."

Jaimie stomped out, muttering how *some* people ignored family loyalty altogether.

Titus was ten years Jaimie's senior, and had always looked out for the lad. It was time for him to let up. Time for Jaimie to act the man.

Bradford was grinning at him.

"You're loving this," Titus said. "You've been trying to saddle me with the job of trustee for months."

"Took a green-eyed wench from across the seas

to convince you of your responsibilities. Wouldn't be surprised if she doesn't lead you a merry chase."

"You've gone and matched her with my brother and you can speak like that?"

Bradford guffawed. His parting words were, "Cracking good sight, you doing somewhat besides licking your own wounds."

"Go to hell, Brad." Old friends could speak bluntly, but there was a limit.

All alone in the quiet parlor, he sat staring into the fire and cursing the day he'd first laid eyes on Madeline Smythe.

5

Now that Madeline had settled in, neighbors called at Esmere Grange and Aunt Almira insisted she and Madeline return the calls.

Esther had reported the servants' tattling that Lady Esmere was making the long-neglected calls to ensure the neighbors' attendance at the prenuptial parties. Even though Madeline had not given the earl an answer, the neighborhood accepted for a fact that a wedding was forthcoming. She supposed they felt as Aunt Almira; what woman in her right mind would refuse an earl?

Madeline made sure Della accompanied them for each visit, much to Aunt Almira's irritation. On one such outing, they met Captain Rhodes in the Leaside village. He rode his gray stallion alongside the carriage and said everything expected of a gentleman.

"One would not detect by his behavior that our niece is nearly betrothed to his brother," Aunt Almira said, obviously miffed when his greeting to her was a mere lift of his hat and a "Good day," before riding on.

On the drive home they passed a great house sprawled at the end of the town. Della explained to Madeline that it was known as the old Hollingsford home. "Captain Rhodes bought it and lives in the wing downstairs."

Since the morning of Madeline's walk with Captain Rhodes, Della had adopted the notion that he would be the perfect suitor for her new cousin. Madeline scoffed, secretly doubting any woman could escape a relationship with the captain with her heart and self intact. For Della's benefit, she pretended disinterest. Nevertheless, Della continuously plotted their visits so their paths might cross, but for several days, they had seen neither the captain nor the earl.

At the luncheon table on one gray and misty day, Della expressed a wish to call at the captain's home in Leaside, but Aunt Almira would have none of it. "Certainly not. He never invites anyone to his house."

Which meant, Madeline assumed, he never invited Almira, so she would not give him the satisfaction of having him not be "at home" should she venture down there.

"And he never comes to call," Almira continued. "He meets Bradford at the Green Dragon for their weekly haunt."

"But he has," Madeline insisted.

"He was present here at the Grange on the day Madeline arrived and he attended our dancing party," Della added.

With thin lips and a steely stare, Aunt Almira said, "Neither instance was a mere neighborly call."

What a pretty woman she is, Madeline thought. If only her disposition matched her looks.

Almira pushed her chair back from the dining table, her teacup rattling in its saucer, and commenced criticizing Della's new hairdo, her scuffed half boots, even the choice of biscuits and sandwiches on her plate.

Madeline put aside her soup spoon. Dare she glance at Della? Her cousin had not uttered a word since her mother's berating lecture began. *Speak up, Della,* Madeline urged. *Say something in your own defense.*

Della's back was as straight as a poker, and her eyes, even though downcast, flashed with rebellion. Madeline could almost see Della's pent-up anger toward her mother. "I am afraid the scuffed footwear is my fault, Aunt. We have been taking long walks on sunny days, and both our boots are suffering."

Almira appeared to ponder what Madeline had told her, and then without warning, without saying a word, she abruptly left them, her skirts swishing as she streamed past.

Madeline hoped this was not a habit of her aunt's, this disappearing when faced with an unpleasant topic of conversation.

Della shifted on the tapestry-covered chair cushion, looking as though she wished she had followed her mother out the door.

The servants had been dismissed to the kitchen. Nothing stirred beyond the fine drizzle rippling down the windowpanes. Madeline was considering how she should break the silence when Della spoke.

"She does love me."

"Yes, I believe she does."

"She is afraid of losing her youthful appearance. Her looks are all she has." She rose and faced Madeline. "She had to marry my father, for the usual reason women must marry quickly, and I do not believe she has ever forgiven herself.

"My father loves me. He raised me as his own. Yet, there are times when I see in his eyes the doubt, the question of whether or not I am of his blood."

What could Madeline say? The daughter was much wiser than the mother. She has a force within her, something inbred that cannot be taught. How wonderful for Jaimie if he should have the good fortune to win her as his countess.

Squire Shields, a local farmer of beautiful pasture-land, threw together a picnic in honor of the earl and his upcoming betrothal. He had his best field scythed, improvised shelters from canvas, ordered races and games for the youngsters, and sent to nearby Torquay for a band.

Madeline and Della arrived early with Uncle Bradford and Aunt Almira. With Esther and the seamstress overseeing her new wardrobe, Della bloomed with confidence and attracted many male admirers. Even her waistline looked a bit narrower, probably due to their treks across the meadows and to the village and back.

As Madeline observed Della posing in the arborvitae with a troop of younger-looking neighbors, she was pleased that Della was enjoying herself, yet she had to remind her cousin more than once of her task to make Jaimie jealous, not merely blush at the compliments bestowed upon her.

Madeline had kept up a constant correspondence with Francesca, who volunteered to sponsor a season in London for Della. Her latest letter hinted that Madeline rush her efforts to see Della introduced into London society. Francesca insisted there was much preparation for this affair; she would need time to write her many friends who had left the city for the summer, and other chaperones would have to be notified.

What a bother this matchmaking!

Jaimie stuck to Madeline's side like clay in rainy weather, so Madeline latched on to Della and they all three trailed about with a bevy of ladies and gentlemen hovering.

They ate the alfresco luncheon and drank the wine and ale. Madeline and Della sat in the shade of their parasols while Jaimie and Mr. Wardton tried to outdo each other with boasting tales of hunting. Madeline had a rapt audience as she spoke of her life at Point Henry and the perils of the war between Britain and North America.

The captain kept his distance, but Madeline caught his gaze on her each time she glanced in his direction, which was often. She knew enough about gentlemen to recognize when one was interested in her. She desperately wanted his attention and felt guilty for the wanting. It would never do. She could not care for one brother while pretending to consider the betrothal of the other.

Prompted by some demon of mischief, she flirted outrageously with each of her admirers in turn. From under her hat, she tossed them looks that gave the impression she had eyes for them alone.

At sixteen she had behaved this way when the young guardsmen of Point Henry had noticed her. But with the captain, it was different.

What about him made her behave in such a forward way?

Della took the hint, followed suit, and soon was swirling in every country dance with a different partner, and to Mr. Wardton she gave two.

Madeline danced with Jaimie and purposely kept her gaze on any gentleman other than him, praising Squire Shields for arranging the picnic.

When Jaimie's answers to her comments finally declined to petulant grunts, she asked if they could watch for a little while. From the sidelines, she launched a full attack. "I notice at society gatherings your close companion, Mr. Wardton, always stands up with Della first."

"How can you say *always*. There have only been the two dancing parties. The one at the Esmere's and this country picnic, which can hardly be construed as a society gathering as you say."

"Oh, but every community has its own polite circles and the social groups here abouts lend credence to gossip when a lady and gentleman are linked more often than not, as are Della and Nicholas Wardton."

He snorted at this. "Della and Nicky? Why, she is a schoolgirl."

"She will soon turn nineteen and is more than ready for a season in London." She let this tidbit sink in, then, "A man wants his bride to have all the social graces, and once Della has town polish, Aunt Almira will not be able to dissuade her suitors. You should know better than any the truth of that, for an earl is a prime catch, and I daresay while you are in town all the ladies primp and smile when you come around."

He smiled briefly at this sneaky compliment, then frowned. "I do not have so many ladies bothering me as you have gentlemen scurrying about."

She tossed her curls and twirled her parasol. "I am so used to attention from the gentlemanly quarter. May I remind you I grew up near a British naval dockyard. My father invited both his army friends and naval officers to our home. Some were as young as I."

Jaimie's eyes narrowed in suspicion. Madeline could well imagine what he thought of her past life in the wilds of Canada.

"The men outnumber the women over there, you know," she continued. "There is no such thing as a wallflower where the British army is garrisoned."

A slight flush colored Jaimie's cheeks and Madeline wondered if she had gone too far.

"I shall keep a sharp eye out for any man who thinks he can—*Ahem,* under my protection you will have no fear of unwanted advances."

Had her ploy had the reverse effect upon him? "I cannot enjoy your protection unless we marry, and you are such a gentleman in demand, it is certain

that you will often be away from home. I understand there are any number of entertainments for
the society gentleman, the boxing matches and the
races, just to mention a few."

"I would expect my wife to accompany me when
I go to London." His brow furrowing, he looked as
though he were considering the ramifications of a
wife encumbering his running loose as he was used
to do.

"I do love the country hours here though. So like
home they are. My friend, Lady Rowe, fair wore
me to a frazzle during my stay with her." She leaned
toward him to whisper, "She informed me that it
was quite acceptable for a married lady to receive
gentlemen callers in her husband's absence."

"Indeed?" the earl's tone dripped with frost.

"I should like to think of you carrying on with
your life as you are accustomed," Madeline said.
"A wife might be a hindrance."

"A wife would not keep me from doing as I
please."

Madeline stared him square in the face. "You
would afford her the same freedom, I presume?"

The earl looked as though he would like to stran-
gle her, and after that they stood in silence for some
twenty minutes for she was afraid to utter another
word.

At the end of one boisterous dance, as if they had
planned it, Della and Captain Rhodes suddenly
appeared before them, laughing, both their faces
pink with the exertion. The captain let slip a loud
whisper, "What a shame we could not have waltzed,
my dear."

Della blushed prettily as she swept him a sweet curtsy.

Jaimie's face flamed. He stomped up to Della and with a peevish voice, exclaimed, "You only stood up with me the once."

Della, bless her, simply smiled as though at a simpleton and walked away toward her father.

Jaimie threw a disgusted look at both Madeline and Della, stalking off to hide himself among the raucous males at the improvised tavern.

With a conspiratorial grin, the captain turned to Madeline. "What have you said to Jaimie? He is holed up over there. One would imagine him to be the fox with the hounds close on his bushy tail."

She laughed. "It struck your brother as unseemly for his *supposed* betrothed to be so merry and popular." The captain might have a suspicion as to what she hoped to accomplish, but she must not own to it, else her scheme would never work. Only Della and Esther knew of the plot, and Della was still skeptical. "I informed him that oftentimes after the marriage vows are spoken the husband and wife both go their merry ways."

"Shocked him, did you?"

"I'm afraid so."

"Pity," he said with a satirical smile.

Very near was a tent scattered around with a collection of tables and chairs. Madeline gazed longingly in that direction, hoping the captain would take the hint. For his sake, she told herself, for the pain he must be suffering was evident in his eyes. She refused two London gentlemen, friends of Jaimie's invited down for the weekend, declaring she must rest.

"Since you are no longer dancing, would you sit with me in the shade?" the captain asked, indicating an empty table for two.

"Yes, thank you. I fear I am parched."

He immediately sent a servant to fetch two glasses of wine, and after settling her in a chair, he eased down beside her, extending his leg.

"Soreness?" she asked. "Exercising the muscles is good, but perhaps not so much as the dancing with Della."

"You are very observant."

The wine arrived and they sipped it slowly, each watching the other.

Finally, as the musicians struck up another merry tune, the captain said, "The village is buzzing with all the visiting you ladies have engaged in of late."

Madeline smiled. "We have had tea under every roof within the Leaside community. My aunt has introduced me to all who would expect me to play the countess."

He said in a low, tight voice, "Of a certainty, I have the notion you want to dissuade my brother from this alliance."

Forcing a shocked expression, Madeline said, "Why ever would you think so?"

"You are prepared to present him with your answer?"

"He has not offered. Yet, since I have been here, I confess I have actually had thoughts of marriage, and of children."

"And?"

"Each time I have those thoughts, I take a liberal

dose of headache powders, and wait for my good sense to return."

He threw back his head and laughed. Many a glance came their way and quizzing glasses were raised. Madeline was satisfied she had caused a stir among the gossips.

"Why, Captain Rhodes. From your reaction, one would think you have a similar opinion of marriage."

"How is it that you know so much about me?"

"I think we both know a bit about what the other is thinking." In spite of herself Madeline imagined what it would be like for this man to love her.

Back at Esmere Grange, Uncle Bradford cornered Madeline at the courtyard entrance after her cousin and aunt had gone inside. "Have you spoken with Lord Hampden about the betrothal?"

She was shocked at his question, for it was more what she had come to expect from his wife. "We have spoken casually of marriage in general."

"Has he formally offered?"

"No, sir."

"Have you given him an opportunity?"

"Uh, perhaps I am not the bride for the earl."

"Pshaw!"

"I would not be surprised if he should declare for Della."

A shadowed look passed over Uncle Bradford's face. "She is a child yet."

"No, Uncle. You've seen for yourself what a

budding woman she is, and she does *so* admire Jaimie."

"Nothing there. Childhood sweethearts is all."

"Have you observed Jaimie's reaction when he sees Della in another man's arms? Dancing, I mean. Why, he is positively livid with jealousy."

The blood in Uncle Bradford's face rose to brighten his forehead. The conversation had definitely taken a turn he disliked. He left her in the doorway with "A month will soon fly by."

The month was racing ahead now.

What was wrong with her? She had a new home and family, new friends, a fortune coming her way as soon as her birth month passed, and a once-in-a-lifetime opportunity with a titled peer of the realm.

What more could a woman wish for?

The answer rocketed to her as she counted the evening stars winking at her.

Captain Titus Evan Rhodes.

6

Each time Madeline descended the stairs in the main hall, she paused before the full-length portrait of her great-grandfather, a tall man with powerful shoulders. Staring at the lifelike figure, she thought how grand he appeared. No exquisitely tailored coat and flowing cravat for him. He wore leather clothing, and the sheathed sword strapped to his hip looked menacing indeed. His black curls were wildly windblown, and she wondered how the artist could have accomplished such a hard and determined facial expression with mere paints. She studied the light in his deep blue eyes, a deeper blue even than Della's.

Beside the rectangular gilt frame holding his bold likeness was a portrait of his son, Madeline's grandfather, whose face reminded her of Uncle Bradford.

There was room for several more large frames, and she thought her uncle must have commissioned his own painting by now.

On this particular day, Madeline wished her great-grandfather were here. Perhaps he would lend some sanity to the whole situation. The household was in a tizzy, as they all had been invited to Hampden Hall for a welcoming-home tea, honoring the earl's mother, who had returned from her travels to Bath. Even the servants would have their own party in the kitchen yard.

Madeline dreaded the occasion, for if the countess was anything like her own mother had been, she would be able to read her true feelings in her eyes.

And then what?

The Esmere family carriage traveled the road up the hill to the crest where stood Hampden Hall with its wooded park. Madeline did not engage in the conversation, as she was preoccupied with the realization that she had seen only a small inch of the vast acres surrounding the earl's home. Lush green fields dotted with sheep lined both sides of the way. Fine shrubs and trees swept down past clear streams that emptied into a large, limpid pond. The road ended at the stables where lanes branched out in all directions, and she wondered which one she had taken on her memorable morning walk with the captain.

Inside the house, the crowning ornaments and decorative knobs repeated the hall's Gothic architecture. Madeline, taking in the splendor around her, knew without a doubt she could never be mistress of such a house. She understood the present countess's abhorrence for the gargoyles and elaborate finials. It was all grand and impressive, but Madeline had led a simple life before coming here and longed for as much in her own future.

The countess greeted the Esmeres with a kind smile and welcomed them to her home. She did not look at all sickly to Madeline. She was medium tall, her face youthful, reminding her somewhat of Lady Rowe, only Francesca was perhaps twenty years younger.

As though reading her thoughts, the countess asked, "How is our friend, Francesca Rowe? I must invite her for a visit."

She then turned to Della and smiled affectionately. "Della dear, you are in excellent looks, as lovely as ever."

Della dropped an exquisite curtsy, murmured her thanks, and kissed the countess's cheek.

Noting real affection between the two, Madeline's heart went out to this gracious lady. Of all the inhabitants of the village and neighbors from the countryside, she had accepted Della's beauty as her due, not something lately discovered. She and the captain had realized it all along.

"Come along, ladies," the countess said. "You must meet my mother, whom I have brought home to live with me in the Dower House. You, too, Almira. It has been years since she has seen you."

Wiry, weathered, and with the appearance of strong bones, Mrs. Artemis Dunn, who was the countess's mother, reminded Madeline of the pioneer women of Kingston. Here was a woman of firm stock, Madeline thought, as she and Della said, "Good day, ma'am."

"The Canadian heiress, eh? Looks English to me." She put out a hand to each of them, and nodded as if confirming her approval. "You look just as you should."

The countess agreed. "Lovely."

Eyeing Almira, who stood behind them, the older lady said, "Almira Esmere, is it not? You look exactly what you are, my dear, a gentleman farmer's wife."

Almira bristled somewhat, obviously not sure whether she had been complimented or not.

Madeline followed the countess around the parlor and was introduced to the elderly country gentlefolk, a number of white-haired ladies and gentlemen who knew everyone's family history and who had married into which family, receiving large, skimpy, or adequate portions and parcels of land. It was a quite different atmosphere from home.

The elegant tea party spilled out onto the terrace when the younger set separated themselves from the oldsters, who were gossiping in loud, good-natured tones in the sunny parlor.

Before Madeline and Della could slip outdoors, Mrs. Dunn beckoned to them. "My daughter thinks I've agreed to live here, but I'll stay only until I'm sick of the place. While I'm at Hampden, you must address me as Grandma'am. The youngsters at home do so."

Madeline thanked her for the privilege. "We're honored."

Grandma'am nodded. "Very proper." Then, gazing

into Madeline's eyes, she said, "Seize your chances. They may not come again."

And to Della: "Always do what is expected of you. It is all important." Her voice just a little lower, "Do not walk in the garden with that Wardton fellow. He ain't at all the thing."

Della went crimson and Madeline swallowed bubbling giggles as the butler announced, "Captain Titus Rhodes."

A thrill coursed along her spine as he entered, the last guest to appear, the only one whom Madeline guessed would dare arrive late.

The countess rushed up to him, looking less ill every minute. "Titus, my dear, I didn't know you were coming. How marvelous. Mother, look who is here," she added as she led him over to his grandmother.

"Humph, bad manners as usual," the elderly lady declared, "You are just like your father."

Yet, Madeline saw that she said it with a definite twinkle in her eye.

"Hush, Grandma'am," the captain said, his own eyes full of laughter. "You were extremely fond of my father."

On the terrace, Jaimie bowed and took Madeline's arm, confessing, "As I am host, I cannot spend every moment with you as I wish."

A few days earlier, she would have believed that wish, but there was a soberness about him she had not noticed previously, and she doubted if he meant the declaration. "I understand, but I shall be devastated nevertheless."

Later, strolling the grounds with him, she watched his effect on the party guests. A good number of the young ladies present gave him flirting glances, and the gentlemen shouldered their way to his side. She supposed that was the way it should be. On this afternoon of blue skies, he was behaving more like the Earl of Hampden should. She hoped he would soon see that an alliance with Della was the suitable one for him.

"You do not care a whit for that boy, yet you behave as though you are disappointed he has not walked three rounds with you in the rose garden as he has with Della and the other ladies."

The voice came from behind her, and she knew in an instant, even before she turned, it was the captain. Shocked at his plain speaking, Madeline really could not think of any decent reply. "I am expected to give him an answer soon."

He laughed deep in his throat. Aware that if she were one of the curious women observing a man like the captain, she, too, would have glanced his way and wondered what could have caused such a wicked laugh.

All earnestness now, the captain said, "It doesn't do for a lady to seem overly willing when a man is about to ask for her hand. Too much eagerness could frighten him away."

"Too much eagerness . . ." Stunned that he could interpret her actions, she confessed, "You are right, sir. I am approaching this task in the wrong way."

"The task. You would welcome assistance?"

"I would indeed, but first, tell me what you assume," she demanded with raised eyebrows.

"I watched you gazing at the surroundings here. The hall is not to your pleasure, am I correct?"

"On the contrary. I find much to please the eye. The estate is beautiful, impressive, grand." She could not say that if she lived here she should feel smothered by such opulence.

His amused look shot through her. "It is possible I could lend a hand in the accomplishment of your goal."

She was dubious. "What do you suggest?"

"Jaimie is so horse mad, perhaps a hunting box, with adequate stables, where they—the couple— could be alone, without all the prying eyes. Or maybe Seascape, the cottage near the sea. All the men in our family have a key to it. There is a magnificent view from the rocks there. Conducive to romance I should think."

"A cottage by the sea! How exciting." She tried ignoring the unspoken dialogue swirling in the air between them. Could he know she plotted for Della's sake and not her own? "The very thing. Thank you, Captain Rhodes. When will you show it to me?"

Titus hadn't thought it necessary to show it to her. His spontaneous plan, hatched at this moment, had been merely to arrange for an outing. But if Miss Smythe wanted to inspect the cottage—what better place to have her all to himself? He wondered if he should offer to send a carriage for her, but decided against it. She seemed more than capable of providing on her own.

Morning dawned sunny and crisp, a fine day for the seaside, yet Titus had the feeling he had been outsmarted. Well aware of the law forbidding a man to marry his brother's wife, he wondered if the law was that binding with a somewhat betrothed miss. No matter. He cared not one whit for matrimony, and certainly not with a provincial who had no inkling of how to go on in London society. But then, he cared nothing about society. He seldom attended the higher echelon's events when he was in town. Maybe a wedding or two. As a rule he amused himself with his army cronies, such officers who happened to be stopping at Stephens's in Bond Street, and with the beautiful courtesans. Yet, there lay in the back of his mind that young man's vision of himself as an older man with a loving wife by his side and a household of youngsters. He supposed every man had that dream at some time or other. Some actually fell into the trap.

But he knew he could not pursue Miss Madeline Smythe; he could think of no good reason to interfere in this hoax of a betrothal. Even though Jaimie seemed indifferent to her, and she with him, many a lasting marriage had come from such an alliance, and Miss Smythe had the ingredients necessary to temper Jaimie's wild meanderings.

Titus crossed his legs on the ottoman, folded his arms across his chest, and stared into the blue flickerings of the coal fire. The question was, should he tell Miss Smythe he had guessed she meant to marry Jaimie off to Della before or after he found a way to have her to himself. To kiss her thoroughly and well meant.

He swore merely to sit back and observe the machinations.

✳   ✳   ✳

Madeline crumpled Della's note and stuffed it into her reticule. She had no time to waste meeting Della, and she most assuredly did not want Della to know what she was about.

Not daring to call for transportation, lest their secret excursion be discovered, Madeline recalled how Della's little maid, Pixie, traveled about the countryside. She arranged with the pretty maid for an afternoon lift to Seascape Cottage.

Madeline smiled as Esther fumed the whole bouncing way along the rutted road in the eggman's wagon. Whispering so Pixie could not hear, Esther said, "The eggman is not what he should be."

Madeline whispered back, "We are not taking up residence with him."

The eggman brought the wagon to a halt on a tree-lined road curving round a cliff, revealing the most charming cottage of bleached boards, sprawling over a grassy lawn with a terrace and potted plants all around. Madeline thought it huge compared to the cottages of Front Street in Kingston. There was no sight of a carriage, and she feared the captain had forsaken their scheme after all.

She was experiencing an instant of regret for her hastiness in coming here when Captain Rhodes and his man, Sheridan, rushed from one of the rustic doors. With barely a greeting, they whisked Madeline and Esther from the wagon, but not before the captain barked strict orders to the eggman and Pixie about returning.

"I should have sent a conveyance for you," he said as he escorted her indoors.

"No, it was better this way." She found herself in the middle of a spacious room with windows all along the back wall, providing an extraordinary view of the sea. A feeling of home, of belonging, came over her. She glanced at the captain and found him staring at her with a look that banished all regret from her mind.

He smiled wryly as he drew her pelisse from her shoulders. "You like what you see."

Turning her back to him, she closed her eyes. "Very much." She'd barely had time to reply when Sheridan brought wine on a tray and, in a discreet dash, returned with some delicious-looking thick sandwiches. Saying how pleased he was to have the company of Miss Esther in his kitchen, he dashed back out again.

At a table set with exquisite crystal dishes, the captain held a chair for her. "We must take a stroll, so that you might see the view."

"But not until these refreshments have vanished." She removed her bonnet and tossed it on a nearby sofa as the captain poured their wine. She tasted it and bit into one of the sandwiches. "Wonderful, Captain Rhodes. I haven't had a bite since breakfast."

"I admire a woman with a healthy appetite." He stared at the honey-colored curls surrounding her face. They'd come loose from the tight knot of braids heaped at the crown of her head. From riding in the wagon, he supposed. "We have been acquainted for an age. When will you call me Titus?"

"I should be honored, but only if you address me as Madeline." She gazed at him over the wineglass while a dark flush rose to her face.

"You and Jaimie have been on Christian name terms from the beginning. His older brother deserves the same consideration." He smiled, wondering what demands she might make on him.

"Too patent, Titus. I'm not that easily charmed."

He knocked over his wine, splashing a spot on his white shirt and riding coat.

After Sheridan had mopped the spill and brought fresh linens, Madeline said, "Speaking of older brothers, it is clearly your duty to deal with Jaimie."

"I beg your pardon?"

"What he needs is more responsibility. More authority in the running of his own estate."

"Tiresome female. How did we arrive at this subject?" Yet he listened. His own thoughts ran along those same lines.

She reminded him, "Young soldiers are given great responsibilities—"

"In the scheme of battle they are not decision makers."

"Facing the enemy has a way of changing a boy into a man."

Her argument was precisely correct. He nodded his agreement. "Watching friends and comrades lose life and limb does more than steady a man's thinking."

"Surely Jaimie could face the fact that overspending could be disastrous for his future?"

Titus pondered that, and she sat and studied him. He marveled that he felt in harmony with this woman. Most generally he liked women who knew how to entertain a gentleman and did not expect a good deal in return. Maybe a gift, or two, or some money to put away for her keeping.

When he was with Miss Smythe, Madeline, his world grew soft around the edges with her in the center as sharp detail. When she was near he lost his ability for tactical maneuvers. Even now, with his well-laid plans, his mind told him to kiss those full lips, caress with his own mouth the dainty curve of her neck.

He rose and drew her to him. She came readily enough, yet he could sense her uncertainty. Beyond holding her hands, he resisted the urge to wrap his arms around her, to crush her tightly against him. His gaze lingered on her bare shoulders.

Consequences be damned.

The groanings and squeaking sounds of a carriage, and the shout of a coachman halting a team outside, made them both stiffen. "Who can that be?" Madeline demanded, incredulous. "Were you expecting someone else? I thought this was a private affair." She ran to the window. "The carriage sitting on the road bears the crest of the Earl of Hampden."

Her presence here with Titus could have every appearance of a lovers' clandestine meeting. If they were found alone in this way, all her plans for the future would be ruined, and her reputation as well. No matter that her maid and his man were about.

"Jaimie will never believe I met you for his sake. Everything is done. Quite ruined."

"I think not," Titus said, but all the while he was

satisfied that others would look upon the situation just as Madeline now presumed. He regretted they may assume he was her lover, but he did not regret the thought they could be lovers.

"Did you set this rendezvous so your brother would think me unfit for his bride? You needn't have bothered, you know. This whole plot is for his benefit, his and Della's. She loves him as I never could, and will make him a lovely and loyal bride. Della shall be the countess he deserves and needs."

"I quite agree." Titus was amused as he knew all along what her plan had been, but nevertheless, he felt culpable, for he had tricked her, and in the way of tricksters, attempted to lay the blame elsewhere. "In truth I was surprised when you came, but then I surmised that both you and your maid are endowed with a great deal of daring so endemic to the women of Canada. You have survived many an atrocity. I don't have to worry about you having the vapors on me."

He glanced out the nearest window, noting that the occupants of the carriage were approaching the terrace. "Even as trouble arrives on our doorstep."

"I have never fainted in my entire life," she declared.

"How is it that only now you are worried? Moments ago you did not seem the least bit skittish about meeting me here alone."

"I am not a green miss, sir. I have been alone with men before. The dark wild forests of home afforded many a walk for courting couples."

"I have heard those stories you told at the squire's picnic—how you and your guardsmen beaux scanned the woods for berries. What kind of proprietary rules can Canada possibly have that a well-born young lady could rendezvous with a man amongst the trees where there is much privacy?"

"You can ask such a question at a time as this?"

As she crossed the room, opening and closing the doors leading into the two wings of the house as though seeking an escapeway, Titus peered out the window at the scowling face of his brother who was peeking in at him.

"Esther accompanies me everywhere, as she has always done," Madeline was expostulating.

"And strolled along with you in the woods, I suppose?"

The abigail appeared at that very moment, with Sheridan close behind. "It is the earl," Esther whispered, "with your cousin, Lady Della." She glared at Madeline as if to say, *Now see what you have done.*

Madeline had the grace to turn bright red. Facing Titus she said, "I am going to faint."

"You only just told me you had never fainted in your entire life," Titus accused.

"I shall faint if I wish!"

Esther rolled her eyes heavenward, and she and Sheridan escaped to the nether reaches of the house.

"Oh, splendid. Esther is abandoning me."

"No one has abandoned you, sweeting." With his attention riveted on the window, Titus slipped his arms around her waist and kissed her bare shoulder.

"How dare you," she declared, but did not pull away. He had the suspicion that she, too, knew Jaimie watched.

He supposed he should look affronted. "I dare because you welcomed my attentions not ten minutes ago."

"We were having a private conversation then."

"Is that what you Canadians call it? How many guardsmen did you say you had seen alone in those wild forests?"

"Hundreds." And with a flounce of her skirts, she went forward to meet Jaimie.

7

Madeline noticed that Jaimie did not bother to pound the door knocker. He crashed the door back and stood on the threshold looking monstrously angry, with Della peering around him as best she could.

Madeline smiled and curtsied, saying, "Good day," in a strangled voice.

Della was no help whatsoever. Her gaze scanned the room, taking in the wineglasses beside the empty decanter, the half-eaten sandwiches, Madeline's curls falling about her face, and the captain's wine-stained shirt. Her shocked silence was deafening.

"Del-la!" Does she think she is staring at a drunken revelry? Madeline wanted nothing so much but to kick her.

Jaimie advanced into the room, his gaze plastered on Titus as though seeing him for the first time. "Suspect you have an explanation?"

"I believe—"

"Oh, cousin, you did make it here," Della cried, cutting off Titus's words.

"Finally you have found your tongue," Madeline murmured.

"Can you ever forgive me for saying such mean things to you?"

"Yes, yes." Madeline wondered what mean words Della had uttered, but she really wanted to know why she and Jaimie were there.

Della tapped her foot in impatience. "I *told* you it was too far to walk."

"By far," but Della's statement only perplexed Madeline more.

Jaimie reiterated. "What *are* you rattling about, Della?"

"We argued about our visit to Seascape. Madeline wanted to walk instead of staying cooped up in the carriage, and by the time your grandmother arrived to bring us here, Madeline was gone."

Madeline barely noticed the fib Della told. "Your grandmother?" She stared at Jaimie. "She is here?"

While Della chattered on, Madeline realized the afternoon drive was the reason Della had left word to meet her. If only Della's note had included the words *Seascape Cottage,* this fiasco could have been avoided. How was she to know the earl's grandmother should choose the same destination, on the very same afternoon?

She faced the captain, shrugging to indicate she had no notion of the ladies' visit, only to find he had the appearance of a man happily engaged in entertainment.

"Della!" Jaimie shouted. "Will you stop that infernal blabbering?"

Della, accustomed to obeying orders rather than giving them, commanded, "Apologize for that. I was trying to restore some sense of reason here."

Jaimie, obviously astounded that she should speak to him in such a way, and in front of others, gave way like a meek kitten. "Yes, of course."

Madeline was impressed, for once started, the earl proved hard to silence.

"Captain Rhodes," Della spoke with such emphasis she could have been on the stage, "you must have happened along to rescue dear Maddie."

"Rescued her, yes, indeed," Titus said with as lascivious a grin as Madeline had ever witnessed.

In the doorway, Sheridan's discreet cough preceded him as he and Esther escorted the earl's mother and grandmother inside.

Jaimie's grandmother glared at him. "What do you mean, leaving your grandmother behind to fend for herself? No sooner than you saw Titus's mount, you ran like a frightened hare!"

Titus brought forth a chair and assisted her, welcoming both ladies and smiling serenely as he did so.

Addressing Sheridan, Grandma'am demanded, "I suppose that smoke coming from the chimney means you have a fire in the kitchen?"

Sheridan assured her he had a splendid fire.

"Then prepare the tea, man." She dismissed him with a wave of her wrinkled hand.

"We brought a basket with us," the countess supplied in explanation. "Had we known you would be here ahead of us, we would not have put cook to the trouble."

"My apologies, Mother." Titus bowed and his smile instantly brought softened and relaxed features to his mother's and grandmother's faces.

Madeline bristled. *A charmer indeed.*

"It's all very well that Titus happened upon you," Jaimie said, his scowling gaze narrowed on Madeline, "but some footpad could have hit you over the head and made off with your valuables."

"Not likely," Titus said. "How often do you run up on a footpad in the wilds? Small pickings in this county for the poorest thief."

"Do not berate the girl," Grandma'am said. "She had the good sense to fetch along her sturdy abigail."

Madeline considered that the welcome end of the conversation about her supposed foolish walk to the cottage. But through the hour that followed, Grandma'am, as Titus and Jaimie also called her, threw Madeline many searching and contemplative glances.

After the tea the countess suggested they go for a short walk around the cliff. Bundled in shawls, Grandma'am announced, "I have seen the sea, thank you." They left her sipping wine and calling for Esther to "Come out of the kitchen and entertain me with stories of that great continent across the ocean."

Jaimie escorted his mother and Della, while Madeline walked with the captain.

Madeline could not say what the view from Seascape really looked like, for she experienced the rest of the day as one drifting through a surreal scene, a dream framed in velvet ribbons. Sunlight followed them, clouds tumbled in the bluest of skies as they covered a sweeping circle back to the cottage. She had come to love these sweet-souled, new friends and their peculiar traits. Except for the captain. She was embarrassed with her reaction to him.

He said little to her as they paused in the stroll, but his manly strength and power commanded her attention. His eyes were indeed dark, shadowed, and questioning.

She returned his gaze and the strident call of the seabirds sounded as though they screeched of caution. She ignored the warning and basked in his look. She had never before known anyone like this man.

All at once the clouds grayed, a fine mist fell, and the wind whipped their clothing.

"My body and soul!" the countess yelped. "Rain again."

"We should have known the sun could not last," Jaimie declared. Sheltering his mother, he quickly ushered her and Della into the cottage.

Titus caught Madeline around the waist, detaining her at the secluded wing beyond the kitchen. She was instantly buried in his arms, and with no protest she surrendered to his kiss. It was soft and gentle, a thrilling contrast to his hard caresses and the unrestrained endearments he murmured.

She had to admit to some fright at his behavior, for she had had no inclination that he would do such a thing. "How daring you are, sir, with your family members on the other side of the wall, within hearing distance if I should call out."

She would not call to them, and he knew it. The scandal of discovery thrilled her as much as the kiss and his intimate contact, and she saw he recognized her excitement.

"Our conversation was interrupted earlier today. You did not have the chance to ask how many women I have met alone. In the forests and about."

In the foggy regions of her mind, she knew the wind was rising; she could hear it rattling the shakes on the roof. But nothing could have shaken her from that spot. Her fingers curled around the rough boards behind her. "You are outrageous, but I suppose I should have expected as much. My mother used to tell me that a gentleman needs practice with many women in order to truly appreciate a fine lady when he finds her."

He chuckled, his gaze alive with roguish lights. "Well done. I acknowledge the hit."

Titus knew Jaimie would come, and when he heard his footstep in the hall, he rose to greet him. He meant to treat him as a man, an equal.

"This has been a day to remember." Jaimie handed his beaver hat to Sheridan, who closed the study door behind him.

"Miss Smythe is not for you, Jaimie."

"How well I know, and do not think me ungrateful for what you've done." He settled back in the brown leather chair and propped his boots on Titus's ottoman. "You carried it off rather well."

Astounded, Titus said, "What?"

"Having her there with you. How did you ever arrange it, brother dear? I saw you staring at me through the window. Wanted to make sure I witnessed an embrace, eh?"

At once Titus suspected a rat in the cellar. Jaimie's tone was too jovial. Titus sat across from him and leaned forward. "You are not telling the whole of the tale."

Jaimie laughed as though they shared a secret joke. "If you could see your face."

"Out with it."

"I overheard you flirting with Madeline in the rose garden at Hampden Hall yesterday."

"The hell you did."

"Are you forgetting the bower where you showed me how to sharpen the tip of my top so we could spike the floor in the belvedere?"

"You wag! What were you doing in there?"

"Waiting for Priscilla Milson. She did not put in an appearance by the way, so I received no kiss as promised. However, I did hear of a plan to rendezvous at Seascape, and thought it a fine spree to join the two of you and bring the matronly bodies of the family along."

Titus swore. "I thought it strange for Grandma'am to come near the place. She's been to the cottage on only one occasion that I know of.

Pronounced it a dull, draughty hole and declared she never wished to visit there again."

In his more familiar tone, Jaimie wailed, "What am I to do, Titus? A month has long since flown by. She expects me to speak for her."

"Do you wish to wed Miss Smythe?"

"I want the life you lead, brother. You answer to no one. I have told Mother there is plenty of time when I am older to beget an heir."

Titus had to agree. "You are one and twenty. Ample time, yet there is still the estate to consider."

"That is at the bottom of the matter." Jaimie sat silent for a moment. "While you were healing, Bradford and Mother hatched this betrothal plot."

Dubious, Titus said, "Mother was in Bath."

"Bradford traveled there as soon as he heard Madeline was on her way, but now you are in charge of the trusteeship, I feel our finances are in good hands. You have taken your two inheritances—"

"One inheritance. The other was Grandma'am's gift. She gave me a portion of her own income."

"The point is you have invested wisely and are comfortably rich, and an envied man. Not merely because you managed to come home from Torres Vedras a hero. Men and women alike admire you for having the means to lord it over us all, yet you live as your station dictates."

"Cut the drama, Jaimie." *While he was healing . . .* while he was feeling sorry for himself was what Jaimie had meant. He had hibernated in a web of despair, accusing himself for the loss of his men and his friend, March. At length, Titus had promised his mother not to pine away his youth, so he had taken on the task of refurbishing the Dower House, paying for repairs out of his own pocket. He had come to Hampden as a ten-year-old when his mother married the old earl. Mending the property was one way he could contribute to the place he had called home for so many years. It would soon be finished, but he could not predict whether she would move unless Jaimie actually took a bride.

"I need your help to make things right, Jaimie. Bradford and the lawyers have done their best, but the outstanding debts must be paid, preferably at once.

"Your father, the earl, spent too much blunt and his fortune is near gone. The estate is producing income, but a mere dwindle of what it should be. Improvements are on the mend, but it shall take some years to carry through and see large profits. Your father was not a manager."

He continued, without an accusatory voice, for the blame lay not with Jaimie. "And you, as his heir, have managed to squander a good deal of capital. In a few months, you and Mother will be living mostly on credit if something is not done. That's one of the reasons I've taken pains to restore the Dower House for her. It will take less expense to run, fewer servants to pay."

Jaimie hung his head. "In future I intend to leave the tonnish whirl of society to the gamers and fops."

Jaimie's words were born more from a sense of duty than desire, and Titus knew it. Smiling he said, "You are young yet for that decision."

"I realize to save the estate I must wed a fortune, and it was Mother's intention that I preserve the line and all that rot." Deadly serious now, he said, "I do not know how this will turn out in the end, for Madeline does have a fortune."

"Della shall receive the same amount."

"How so? She is not the true—"

"Never say it, man. She is Bradford's own blood."

Jaimie nodded. "I believe you know what you are talking about."

"And Della is the very one who will stand up to your spoiled ways. She has followed you in many a rompish lark."

Jaimie looked him straight in the eye. "How can I shed this trap they have set for me?"

Titus asked, "Does Miss Smythe suspect your feelings?"

Sheepishly, he replied, "Waiting for the right moment to approach her."

"There is no right moment. Tell her the truth."

"I'm not sure I have the courage."

Titus smacked him on the back. "I have every confidence in you, brother."

After an hour or so, Jaimie said farewell and started for the door, but he doubled back. "You do know if I loved her I would have called you out?"

"No doubt in my mind."

His little brother had grown up at last.

Madeline's swift and impetuous response to the captain's kiss at Seascape had left her feeling strange and extraordinary, apart from the world. She refused to dwell on what he might think of her, but wondered instead how he had spent the days since. Despite his behavior when Jaimie and the others had arrived at the cottage, she knew in her bones what she felt for him.

And that realization prompted her to speak immediately to Jaimie. She had made plans to meet him at precisely three o'clock at the belvedere near the pond, a short walk from the Esmere stables.

As she tiptoed down the stairs, she sighed in relief, for she could hear Della in the drawing room practicing the pianoforte. She'd had a difficult time avoiding her, but was determined the meeting be a private one. Gentlemen, especially one as high in the instep as the earl, could not abide rebuffs. She vowed to break the news to him as gently as possible, but was not worried about his reaction. A woman knows when a man ceases his adulation for her.

At the foot of the stairway, she ran into her uncle. "Oh, Uncle Bradford, do look at the resemblance of Della to Great-Grandfather." Taking his arm, she walked back up to the first landing with him and gestured toward the portrait. "Have you ever seen anything so uncanny? I know he must have been a rugged individual, and Della is so feminine, but just see? Their hair, the same wild curls, black as soot, and no one has eyes as blue as these. Almost violet. Save Della, of course."

"I always thought her coloring came from her mother," Uncle Bradford said, somewhat in awe as he gazed at the painting.

"Aunt Almira? No, her dark hair has streaks of henna. Della's is as black as the coal pile. Even her facial features are the same as Great-Grandfather's.

See here?" She traced the baron's dark brows. "Della is always wailing that she should shave them off, her brows I mean. She finds them masculine-looking, but many ladies must paint on eyebrows."

"I see," Uncle Bradford murmured.

She stood back, holding on to her uncle's arm, keeping him there. "How lucky Della is to have inherited Great-Grandfather's sharp features, and I have told her so." She had not mentioned anything of the sort to Della but saw that she must, and in Almira's presence.

She lingered a little longer. "Uncle Bradford?"

Distracted by the portrait, he murmured, "Yes?"

"I do not wish to marry Lord Hampden. I shall tell him so, and I feel he will be relieved."

He faced her then. "Are you sure?"

"Oh, yes," she answered emphatically. "Jaimie needs and deserves a true English bride, one who will care for his duties and responsibilities."

"I respect your honesty."

She wanted to stay and truly convince him Della was his offspring, but she simply could not. Jaimie was waiting.

"Since I have known you, and come to respect you . . ." She faltered. How to say the words. "I have grown to love you as a brother."

Jaimie gasped and Madeline's heart lurched. She could not bear to think she could hurt him after all. She rushed on before losing her nerve altogether. "It is an honor even to consider the possibility of an alliance between us, but I could never marry you."

He drew a linen square from his coat and wiped the perspiration from his brow. "My dear lady—"

"Wait, hear me out. There should be a charge as explosive as a battery of cannon fire between two people contemplating matrimony. With me, Jaimie, you simply would have no chance for even a fizzing squib, it's not possible. I adore the plain and simple affairs of life. Just think how bored you would be."

"Doubt any man could find boredom in your presence."

She ignored the incredulous look lighting his face. "Now take an unrestrained girl like Della; she would lead you a merry chase."

"Titus has predicted the very same."

"Really? Heed him, as a former captain in the British army it is a certainty he has been the rounds."

"That he has. I could tell you some tales."

She drew herself up as straight as the timbers supporting the ceiling of the belvedere. "I'm sure I don't want to hear of them." In fact, the remark rankled.

He actually blushed. "I'm forgetting myself."

She pondered whether or not to mention that Uncle Bradford should be delighted to have him as his son-in-law but decided against it. One thing at a time.

"Do forgive me. You are not accustomed to such messages from the ladies of your acquaintance, but I felt I had to inform you. I could not have you expecting what can never be." She hoped she was not heaping it on too abundantly.

Jaimie's face revealed relief and Madeline discovered his deep laugh sounded exactly like Titus's.

Ah, she thought, some maternal ancestor had been a wicked rogue indeed. "You don't have to sound *so* relieved."

He swept her an elaborate bow. "My apologies, dear lady. Just my way of hiding a broken heart."

Madeline sensed he was as glad as she to be shed of the whole situation. The giggles inside her bubbled over at his comical expression.

Jaimie took her arm and they walked along the banks of the pond. He asked, "What do you think of Titus?"

Sharp apprehension tingled through her. "The captain is an interesting man."

"Oh-ho, interesting is he? In what way?"

"All right, he is dangerous. The sort concerned mothers warn their daughters to avoid."

"What's this? Titus is a fine chap. Treats Mother and Grandma'am with the greatest respect."

"He's not likely to court either of them, is he?"

He laughed heartily at first, then, "Am I, too?" The question he blurted was too eager.

"Dangerous? Oh, yes, a lady must be very careful."

"You felt safe enough to meet me at the belvedere," he answered with indignance. "What about yesterday? Were you uncomfortable at Seascape before we arrived?"

She could not answer that question without revealing her feelings, and should he ask if she had met Titus deliberately, she had no intention of admitting it.

Turning to face him, she declared, "It just occurred to me that while we were strolling at Seascape, you were very attentive to Della. Do you suppose if you and I pretended to admire each other, that Della might pay closer mind to you?"

He merely stared.

"I mean to say, when a lady lavishes attention on a gentleman, that usually generates much renewed interest on the part of other ladies." She knew she should not speak so familiarly with him, and his surprised look said as much. But the two of them had minutes ago put an end to their own alliance. Surely they could plot together.

He gave her a conspiratorial grin. "I should be delighted to engage in a game of romance."

She thought it best to change the subject now that she had accomplished her objective. It would be foolish to play games with no witnesses about.

"I confess that my ardor for you had cooled somewhat, but now I see my mistake." He bowed low over her hand. "As you have flamed my heart, I shall be your servant always."

What did he mean by that? "Please, let us speak of a less intimate subject on such a beautiful day as this."

"You will never lack for an escort. I will call at the Grange often."

There was an uneasiness in the pit of her stomach growing more painful with every word he uttered. "I shall be quite safe from here, Jaimie. Do go back. Your horse should be itching for a good stretch."

He looked around. "Are you quite sure?"

She nodded, flinging her arm at a stand of trees on the opposite side of the rillet. The water shone silvery in the sunlight. "Esmere Grange is right across the bridge there."

"I'll leave you then."

And they parted, Madeline swearing to herself that she should have spoken more adamantly. She should have demanded that he speak to Uncle Bradford and disclaim the alliance.

She watched him out of sight and started off at a quick stride when she heard hooves thundering close behind her. Turning back, she was startled to see the captain, and not Jaimie as she expected. On his gray stallion, he seemed larger and even more intriguing, though his blue coat and buckskins were normal fare.

He reined in just off the path where she stood watching him.

"Alone again?"

"Not really. I've just left Jaimie. We were at the belvedere."

"His protective concern of ladies walking alone does not extend beyond yesterday, I see." He dismounted, widening the grin on his face. "I shall escort you home, if you will allow me?"

"It is quite unnecessary, I assure you."

"Oh? Your abigail is lurking about in the trees, is she?"

This said with a casual, intimate smile. Madeline knew a number of those could render her lost to all good sense. "What an odious man you are."

Holding the prancing gray's reins, he laughed. "Would you say odious is several notches below dangerous, or does your measure go the other way?"

She simply stared at him in incredulous silence.

"Voices travel across water, did you know?"

"You eavesdropped on our private conversation."

"Having another one of those, were you?"

"Are you a teasing man by nature, or do you work at it?"

"I make it a point to practice when you are around," he said with a smile. "Shall I carry you home?"

"Certainly not."

"Very well," he answered with indifference. He put one booted toe in the stirrup, threw his other leg over the horse's back, gave her a sharp military salute, and galloped off.

8

Madeline ground her teeth together as she turned her back on the departing captain. She swore he could not unsettle her, yet kicking at pebbles did nothing toward squashing her disappointment.

She crossed the footbridge spanning the stream that separated the ancestral acres of the two estates. Aunt Almira's quavering and tearful voice drifted from the direction of a stone bench on the other side. Alarmed, she rushed forward and overheard a conversation of a serious matter indeed.

"Then why did he convince his grandmother not to settle the granddaughter's portion on Della?"

"What gabster have you listened to? I do not believe he did any such thing."

There sat the countess consoling Almira, whose face was splotchy from weeping.

"Oh, Aunt," Madeline said, in a worried voice, "I do not wish to intrude, but has something happened? Has there been an accident?"

Della stood apart, wringing her hands. With an anxious look, she ran to Madeline, "It is all my fault."

The countess gestured for Della to keep quiet, but Almira said, "What does it matter if she knows? Everyone speaks of it."

Tucking her handkerchief into her sleeve cuff, the countess announced, "Della has confronted her mother with the issue of her birth," which set Almira's tears off again. "Come, Almira, do. No one believes that old tale. Bradford loves his daughter. Why, she is an Esmere to the core."

Reflecting on Almira's acerbic personality, Madeline found this pitiful heap of tears upsetting. The scene proved her mother's words that grumpy and hateful persons needed love more than any.

"We must *do* something," Della wailed in a tone loud enough to scare away the birds.

Madeline knelt before Almira, taking her hands. "Ma'am, Della is the very image of Great-Grandfather."

Almira studied Madeline with interest. "I have often thought the same. The point is Bradford must be brought to see it."

"Have you never said as much to Uncle Bradford?"

Almira frowned and shook her head.

Madeline barely hesitated. "This very afternoon Uncle and I discussed the portrait of Great-Grandfather on the grand stairway. He agreed with me how like the old man Della appears." She glanced to Della. "You are lucky to have inherited his handsome features."

"There's no denying family traits," the countess added with emphasis.

What mischievous imp prodded Madeline to say what came out of her mouth next, she did not know. "He loves Della, 'tis true, but I have seen the adoring glances he passes your way, Aunt. He must be very much in love with you."

At those words, Almira's face transformed magically. She dried her tears and straightened her shawl. "Well, he is a dear man."

"There," the countess said, passing a look of smug satisfaction to Madeline. "Bradford is a man who knows his duty." She reached for Madeline's hand. "Walk with me to the house, for I must run along."

With a gleam in her eye, Almira allowed Della to lead her toward the terrace.

Madeline and the countess followed behind.

"Very wise, my dear," the countess whispered. "Very wise, indeed."

Madeline caught her breath at the countess's smile. It was an exact replica of the captain's lascivious grin.

Midweek at the Green Dragon was usually quiet and uneventful, but the downpour of late afternoon had left the roads near impassable. The parlor where Titus and Bradford held their gentlemen's evening out was let to a traveling family of eight.

Titus sat at a corner table in the dining room listening to the proprietor apologize for his wife's misjudgment. "She should have saved the private room for our regular customers. She knew you would be stopping in, sir."

"Leave it alone, Hiram, and bring my dinner."

The diverting afternoon spent at Seascape had left Titus with tender feelings that were gradually replaced with a tormenting irritation toward Miss Madeline Smythe. He was all too aware his reaction was illogical, his reasoning twisted. Her arrival in the neighborhood had thrown a clinker into his former melancholy existence. He had spent weeks in solitary isolation, thoroughly enjoying his recuperation, wallowing in self-pity, overwrought with the results of a battle that he could not control. March, blind fool, would have met death no matter the circumstances. Titus knew this, had always known it, but blaming himself absolved his guilt about having followed March willfully, and without compunction, until, that is, the report of the numbers of dead and wounded infantrymen lay crumpled in his hand.

As Hiram, large and silent, served the dinner, Bradford said, "Strangest thing has occurred."

Titus sipped his ale and said nothing, waiting.

Bradford sat distracted, staring into space.

Titus bore the silence as long as he could. Cursing the weather and his new task as trustee for Hampden, annoyed with the world in general, he clunked down his mug. "Don't keep me on tenterhooks, man, what has happened?"

At first Bradford seemed to have forgotten what he meant to say, then, "This afternoon Madeline called my attention to the similarities of appearance in the portrait of Grandfather and Della."

"Go on." Bradford had a light in his eyes Titus had seen before, usually when a man discovered he was in love.

"She pointed out the family features between the two. There is no doubt they are related. It's uncanny, the bone structure, and especially the hair and eyes."

"Pattern cards. I've always thought so." Titus dipped into the stew. "Better eat, it's growing cold."

When Bradford said nothing and sat as though pondering the matter further, Titus groaned. "Never say you have not considered it before?"

"I've been so positive that Almira was untrue. I love Della, you know that, but to discover she is, after all, my very own blood." Bradford drew out a large linen square and blew his nose.

Titus pushed away his bowl. His friend was clearly touched by Madeline's observations. "You love your wife, Brad."

"Yes, yes, I do." He dug into the meal then with gusto. "Almira can be shrewish at times, and she's a fripperies buyer, but—"

"So? You could not abide a bluestocking, or a leader of fashion who demanded to live most of the year in London."

"How well I know." He glanced across the noisy dining room as though just now aware of his surroundings. "I had the chance to marry Francesca, you know. I didn't do the offering. She asked me, before you and I were off to Spain."

For a certainty Titus knew. On Bradford's wedding day he'd had to console Francesca, dry her tears, and coax her from the house where she'd sworn to remain and never marry. "Why didn't you? Francesca was all the crack. Rich, too."

"Like a sister to me," Bradford said between bites. "A dasher, I know, but not the same as with Almira."

"Go away with her, Brad. You really never had a wedding trip."

"Away? Where would we go?"

"Why to Bath, or no, to Brighton. It's rumored that Prinny grew uncomfortable living in his bow-fronted house with its shallow dome. His followers are flocking there to discover what elegant improvements Holland had designed."

Bradford looked up. "I have not been there but once myself, and Almira does love that sort of folderol."

Titus marveled that his coldhearted opinion of Almira had thawed a bit. Probably due to Jaimie's information that Almira was not the one who had instigated the betrothal between Jaimie and Madeline. He was turning softhearted in his old age. Softheaded, more like.

They discussed the farming problems of the Hampden estate: outbuildings, roofing, and the like. Titus was relieved that Bradford approved of his purchase of proper roof tiles.

The home farm's two bailiffs, father and son, were competent men who worked well together and followed orders with a pride for detail. All they needed was direction, and at present the money to repair buildings that lay in neglect. A man's hands were tied if he owned acres of land without the means to maintain them.

"When do you think we should go?" Bradford asked.

"Where?"

"To Brighton."

"I thought we were off that."

"Who will stay with the young ladies? Almira wouldn't stand for sending them to Hampden."

"Why not?" Titus demanded with some umbrage. "Extraordinary chaperones, my mother and Grandma'am."

Bradford looked askance at Titus. "I trust Jaimie in the same household, but too much temptation is more than some males can stand."

"Speaking of yourself, are you?" He could not resist the taunt.

Bradford scowled. "At least I married her, which is more than some gents we both know."

Teasing ruthlessly now, Titus said, "I think you planned it that way on purpose."

"Have done!"

Titus knew when to cease the twitting. He and Bradford were friends of old, but he would not overstep his bounds. "We shall invite Francesca. Mother mentioned it not many days ago, when she came home from Bath." He set his lips in a grim smile, for he had written Francesca back in June, warning her to prepare for a summons. She had sent a quick reply, providing the address of one of her late husband's country estates where she would be residing for the summer.

This was working out better than if he had planned it all himself.

*   *   *

Madeline's first instinct was not to inform Uncle Bradford of her talk with Jaimie, then she decided she must. She feared Jaimie would not speak of it at all. His strange behavior had unnerved her.

Common sense urged her to seek a life of her own, away from Leaside, but not too far away. Now that she had grown to know and admire her mother's family, she wished to keep in contact, but she could not help feeling like an intruder. She realized she might always feel that way. She had not grown up at the Grange, and despite her affection for family members, she could not feel totally at home here. If she remained, she would be under Uncle Bradford's protection, and she was too independent for that kind of life. "Our stay here is temporary, Esther."

The maid paused in the folding of linens, glancing over her shoulder at Madeline.

"We can fend for ourselves; we led a much simpler life at home, and we can do it once more."

"It won't be an easy matter, just the two of us. 'Twould have been less of a task had we stayed in Canada."

Madeline smiled. As a girl she had learned that Esther's sharp tongue was more bark than bite. "I have some money, that and the inheritance from my great-grandmother shall keep us until we establish some proprietary means of earning income."

"When do you plan to have at this new venture?"

Madeline released a resigned sigh. "I shall have to think on it."

"Have a care. Parting can break your heart."

9

Madeline stepped out of the warm, verbena-scented water of her bath and wrapped a large towel around her. As a girl, her mother had used the same slipper tub in this very room. What luxuries she had relinquished to follow her love in his military career. Madeline thought she knew how easy that would be, for a woman to follow the man she loved, and who loved her in return.

Her family's life had been easier than most in Kingston, but both Madeline and her mother had known days when they alone had to cope with the problems of running a house, and most especially with the cooking and baking. Servants came and went, for after they saved the wherewithal to purchase a piece of land, they did not stay around to serve a master.

Even though Esther and the house staff here at Esmere Grange waited on her, Madeline took an active role in caring for herself. To rely on others for her least whim seemed silly and exorbitant.

Given his behavior this past week, the captain would surely attend the dinner party this evening, and it was important to Madeline that she look her best. She dressed in a soft cream gown cut low, with a pink silk overskirt stitched in fine embroidery tied over that, and swathed about her shoulders a gauzy shawl of Damask rose.

The servants were whispering about the lord and lady of the house, and there was a distinct expectation of excitement in the air. Uncle Bradford and Aunt Almira's attitude toward each other had visibly altered in the last few days, and Della had alerted the guests that her father had mentioned a surprise. Recalling her first evening in the house, Madeline prayed this new development did not concern her.

Refusing to allow the Seascape misadventure to haunt her, Madeline faced the captain across the dining table and graced him with one of her beguiling smiles.

He returned it with a mysterious grin that brought a vivid image to mind—his gaze, dark as midnight, when he'd bent his head and kissed her.

Not one to flee in the face of danger, she conversed first with his grandmother to her right, then with Jaimie on her left. When Jaimie turned away to speak with his hostess, Madeline fingered the delicate Brussels lace bordering the tablecloth.

"What a long night ahead of us if you insist on

studying the table lace," Captain Rhodes said in a low voice.

She gave him a haughty look. "I understand it is inexcusably rude to converse across the table."

"I've never known anyone in this small community to observe that foolish rule."

She surveyed the others at the table who appeared occupied with their own conversations. "I'd venture to say you are a master at rule breaking."

"Would you care to put that statement to the test? After dinner, of course."

Her heartbeat quickened, but she dare not look away. "I believe Della has invited Priscilla Milson's visiting friends over for music and dancing. Della has convinced her mother that everyone waltzes, and Aunt Almira has relented. She has given the couples permission to practice in the music room.

"Perchance, Captain Rhodes, you will find a willing participant among the guests. After dinner, of course."

"Another clever retort, Miss Smythe."

Madeline's throat tightened at his amused tone. From the beginning she had thought him intriguing rather than handsome. Tonight he looked splendid in evening clothes. His black jacket matched his dark pirate's heart, and she had to admit the man had her in a temporary state of madness.

As soon as the wine was poured, Uncle Bradford stood. "I should like to propose a toast to my wife of nineteen years. I name it a wedding toast, as we are taking our long overdue wedding trip."

"Papa!" Della said into the shocked silence.

Then with shuffling feet and much speculating

dialogue, all but Almira and Grandma'am arose. As the company drank to the host and hostess, Madeline glanced at the captain and broke into a quiet ripple of laughter. "I see you are not surprised." What an obtuse thing to say, and she could not blame it on the wine. She'd had only one sip.

He gave her a startled look, then admitted, "Not at all."

"*Well?*" Della could contain herself no longer. "Mama, where will you go? How long will you stay?" She glanced accusingly at Madeline. "Did you know about this?"

Madeline pursed her lips. "Hush, Della. This is a surprise to me as well." Everyone was waiting for Almira to speak.

"To Brighton, I think," Bradford supplied, "or Bath. The choice is yours, my dear."

Almira blushed like a schoolgirl and gestured for her guests to sit. Facing Bradford, she said, "Brighton will do very well. Wherever you choose, dear, is fine."

Grandma'am announced with strong finality that Bath was the only choice. "The hotels in Brighton are clean and roomy enough, but too noisy. They cannot compare to a private residence." She gave Jaimie a steely stare. "The earl's fashionable address in Bath is exactly right for a wedding trip."

Jaimie, who had spoken few words up to now, agreed, saying, "Extraordinary idea, Bradford. Please accept a key to our house there. Grandma'am will see that it is ready for you."

Titus cleared his throat and ventured, "Mother and I have invited Lady Rowe for chaperoning the young ladies."

Della's astounded "Oh!" and her mother's quiet gasp blended with Grandma'am's snort.

"You have to rise early to best Frannie," Grandma'am said. "She's a sly one. Nabbed herself a rich viscount in her first season, and was only married for two years before he inherited his father's title of earl. Then he stuck his spoon in the wall."

In quiet tones Lady Hampden informed Madeline that Francesca's childhood home was near Leaside, north of Torquay.

Madeline was relieved to hear they expected her to arrive in the next few days. A visit from Francesca; just the distraction necessary for ridding her mind of Captain Titus Rhodes. The invitation must have been speedy, for Francesca had not mentioned a visit in her last letter.

"I wonder if she will bring servants with her, or depend upon help from the village?" Almira asked.

Lady Hampden smiled at Almira. "No need for her to open her old home. The summer is near over and Bradford has said she may stay at Esmere Grange. I would love to have her at Hampden Hall, but you know how Jaimie and his friends run loose around the house, and since she is to chaperone, we did not find it advisable to have the young ladies and gentlemen under one roof."

"How busy you have been." Almira looked vexed that they had plotted without her knowledge. "We will give her the front bedroom near Madeline's."

*   *   *

Titus grinned at Bradford as Jaimie left his half-empty glass on the dining room table. The Milson party was arriving in the corridor, and Della's high pitch of excitement caught on, pell-mell. The eight young ladies and gentlemen flooded the house with jumbled footsteps, laughter, and squeals of delight.

Bradford chuckled and capped the empty decanter beside him. "Della has probably informed them she'll be a free spirit once her parents are on the road to Bath and out of sight for two weeks."

Nodding, Titus followed his host out of the dining room.

"Let us sneak in by the back," Bradford said as he swung open a door to the long narrow chamber that led into the music room where the rest of the company were assembled.

Formerly a waiting room, the billiards room was lined with bookshelves and overstuffed chairs. In the center stood the carved-leg, felt-covered table that was the source of the room's name. "We cannot escape the party, Bradford," Titus said. "You are the host, you know."

"With Almira, Lady Hampden, and your grandmother properly chaperoning the young ones, I should be allowed some respite."

"Try and seek it, if you can." Nowadays the billiards room was where the gentlemen played cards or smoked, so they would not have to leave the house in reverence to ladies present.

"Demme, but I am itching for this journey," Bradford declared. "Since Madeline's arrival, there is a new venture round here every hour. I cannot wait to depart."

Titus strolled over to the connecting wall that supported two wide alcoves leading into the larger music room. He recalled the many children's parties he had attended there, while the grownups watched from this quieter place. Della, seated at the pianoforte, was waiting for Jaimie to turn the pages of the music. He could not see Madeline from this point, but noticed Nicholas Wardton among the gents. "That scamp Wardton is here."

"I thought Jaimie sent him packing after the squire's picnic."

"He did, after finally deciding for himself that Wardton was a hanger-on, flitting from one household to the next. He must have finagled an invite to Priscilla Milson's party."

"That is easy enough to do. Cannot have an uneven number at table, you know," Bradford said in reference to the many social rules the two of them often ridiculed.

Titus laughed softly. "Della is looking lovelier than ever. It has been good for her, having Miss Smythe here."

"I agree, hardly recognize Della these days."

Titus moved near the other gilded alcove and rested an elbow on a shelf where he could watch Madeline. Her prettiness evolved from her vixenish personality and a compelling magnetism that drew gentlemen to her. It was a way she had, her coquettish gaze when she tilted her head to look at a gentleman, or her soft, golden laughter that spread through a man's body like rays of sunshine. Her mannerisms were not immodest, yet so alluring there was instant response from every male who happened near. It was

as natural as her habit of brushing the wayward ten-
drils of hair behind her ears.

But beyond that, she had unwavering independence and a boldness to face whatever life handed
her. He couldn't help admiring her.

"I say, Titus, did you hear?" Bradford raised his
voice above the twanging of the music and the solid
ivory billiard balls clanking together. "Our Canadian
niece has no wish for a handle to her name. Told me
so. Turned down the alliance with Jaimie."

Caught off guard, Titus said, "Jaimie, also, is
hesitant."

"That so?"

"Hmmm, we've spoken of it somewhat." Titus
spoke casually, wondering if he was fooling
Bradford with his offhand comment.

"Ye-es," Bradford took careful aim with his cue.
"Madeline says Jaimie needs a true English lady for
his bride."

"I have to agree then, and no harm has been
done. Notices have not been published in the news-
papers, no banns read."

Bradford straightened from his bent position.
"You sound relieved yourself."

Titus walked over and picked up one of the ivory
balls, tossing it from one hand to the other. "And
right under our noses is the most likely candidate."
He nodded toward the music room where furniture
had been moved to allow for dancing. Della, still at
the pianoforte, was playing and singing. "Della is
prettier and as lively as any of the other young
ladies Jaimie sees on a regular basis."

Bradford nodded. "She is not so plump as before."

"Baby fat. Losing it, I'd say." Titus released the ball onto the green surface and chose a stick, feeling its tip. "My stepfather was forever speaking of joining the bordering estates."

Bradford stood with his stick resting on the floor, the heavier end of it between his shoes, listening.

"Beyond that, Della was the apple of his eye. He bounced her on his knee and brought her as many sweets and gifts from London as he ever did Jaimie."

"I remember." Bradford laid down the stick and stared through the alcove at the couples singing along with the music. "Della is a beautiful young lady, is she not? And I have been a blind fool."

"Where women are concerned, we males often make fools of ourselves."

Madeline sat with Lady Hampden and Grandma'am, watching Della and the petite Priscilla Milson compete at the pianoforte, each basking in the praise of the gentlemen and other young ladies in the party.

After the first few songs, she could not help but notice that the captain's glance, even as he played billiards, was constantly settling upon her. Each time she looked his way, she caught a glint of pleasure in his eyes. It was difficult to observe the party without including him in her gaze, yet his attention perturbed her. She had even gone so far as to turn on the small sofa so that she no longer faced the larger group.

The local population might consider her a

provincial, but she was no fool. She had had enough of these flirtatious glances before to know what lay behind them.

Grandma'am was saying to her daughter, "Francesca Rowe will do the correct thing for these young ones, that she will. Frannie knows well which gentlemen to encourage and which to turn away." She bent over Madeline to look pointedly at Nicholas Wardton.

Grandma'am had never approved of Mr. Wardton, and Madeline wondered if it was only because of his impoverished condition. She did not feel the elderly lady would condemn a man merely because he had no resources.

As there was no forthcoming comment, Grandma'am continued, "Della must needs wipe that scowl from her face."

Madeline glanced at Della, who did indeed have an unpleasant expression on her face. Madeline smiled. Of late, Della had grown used to the attentions of various gentlemen, and was clearly upset over the adulation Jaimie was showering on Priscilla.

"She has not learned to hide her true feelings. The attention given Priscilla rankles," Madeline whispered, deciding to rescue Della before her impetuous personality exploded. "I shall offer assistance."

She crossed the wide room just as Priscilla drew her piece to a close. "You must relinquish your place to me, ladies. I will attempt to play a waltz so the dancing can commence, or we shall lose some of our gentlemen to billiards. They have been eyeing the green felt through the alcove there."

Faces turned to catch the captain and Uncle Bradford standing in the alcove, talking, the rectangular table behind them.

Lady Hampden rose and swept across the polished floor, her satin gown whispering in the sudden silence. "I detest sitting on the sidelines and watching the dancing. *I* will play a waltz. You youngsters nab your partners, for I cannot sit idle another minute."

"How kind," Madeline said.

Della dipped into a deep curtsy, showing great respect to the earl's mama. "Thank you, Lady Hampden."

Lady Hampden played prettily, and if she missed a few chords, no one noticed.

Madeline loved the waltz and smiled at the other couples rotating past. She danced with all the gentlemen except the captain, congratulating herself on her successful attempts at avoiding him.

After a midnight supper, Uncle Bradford clapped his hands and called for a general breakup of the party. "Lady Hampden is fair worn to a frazzle!"

The couples registered good-natured complaints, and Jaimie declared, "I don't know about you other fellows, but I do need the practice."

This was met with laughter and Della volunteered to play one last tune, announcing it a waltz set to a slower beat. "For those with more than two feet."

Madeline knew her well enough to recognize she had added that last for Jaimie's benefit, as he had chosen Priscilla for his partner.

Captain Rhodes was standing barely two feet away from Madeline, one corner of his mouth tilted in a smile. Resigned to waltzing with him, she stepped a half turn away, but she could avoid him no longer without appearing grossly impolite.

"Come now, Madeline, a waltz with me cannot be all that bad."

At that familiar, intimate voice, Madeline whipped around, her ivory gown rippling into folds about her ankles.

The captain faced her, white shirt front gleaming. With a swift step he shouldered one of the younger gentlemen aside. "I believe I have this waltz."

He bowed and Madeline forgot about Della and Jaimie. She went into his arms for the second time in a few days.

"I saw that jackanapes fixing his hungry eyes on you. Teach him a thing or two about how to go on in polite company." This he growled out as the music commenced.

Madeline laughed. "You do say the most absurd things."

With his dark and rugged face looming above her, she thought it outrageous how appealing she found him. She vowed, once again, not to recall his mouth on hers. And once again she failed. Thoughts of him tumbled inside her head. His hand at her waist conjured up images of his caresses, and of their searing impact. No man had ever made such an impression on her.

The waltz came to a close, and amid the dancers' chorused denials that the evening had to end, she drew away from him, pressing her hands to her burning cheeks. Her throat tightened as she said, "Good night, Captain Rhodes."

"Your servant." He bowed formally. "It has been a great pleasure."

At the threshold he turned, giving her one of his salutes.

Indeed, Esther was correct. Leaving here would surely break her heart.

10

   While Uncle Bradford directed the loading
of the carriage, Almira asked Madeline to unclasp
the strand of pearls around her neck. "I want Della
to wear them to the assembly on Friday evening.
See that she wears her new yellowish gown with the
tiny pearls sewn in the bodice."

   "I couldn't, Mama. Those are your favorites,"
Della declared, backing away.

   "Be still, Della," Madeline urged, holding the necklace solicitously. "Just let me fasten the pearls about
your neck and perhaps you will change your mind."

   Surprisingly, Della held her off, saying, "No, I
cannot."

   At last it was Almira who said, "Take the pearls,
Della, do. Maddie shall taunt you the entire week if
you do not."

It was Almira's use of Della's pet name for her that convinced Madeline her aunt truly meant for Della to have the necklace. With raised eyebrows she approached Della once more.

Della relented, and when Madeline saw the strand of pearls on her cousin's white skin, she ran upstairs and fetched her own pearl earrings. Secured at the base of each tiny earring was a single pear-shaped diamond exactly like the one at the center of the pearl necklace.

"They are a perfect match," Madeline said as Della attached them to her earlobes.

"And why not? They were a set," Almira offered. "Your grandmother wore them at her wedding—a gift from her husband's mother. She gave them to your mother, Madeline, but for some reason Hilda left the pearls behind when she departed for Canada."

"Yes, I remember she told me once the earrings had belonged to her mother. How Mama cherished them." She took a quick breath, drawing strength from that memory. "So, Della, they are now reunited, and you will wear the set to the assembly. In that way, we'll honor the women of our family."

After her aunt and uncle departed for Bath, Madeline sat in the dining room having a late breakfast alone, when Della burst into the room, slamming back the doors.

"How dare you keep a secret from me," Della fumed, waving her riding crop.

"What . . . what secret?"

"You refused Jaimie's offer."

Madeline frowned. "He hasn't offered."

"You told him you didn't wish to wed him."

"How did you find that out?" Madeline had related to Della none of the details of the defunct betrothal, and now realized her mistake.

"Jaimie said as much this morning while we were out riding. He told me you weren't quite ready to give an answer. I always have to make inquiries around here if I want to know what's going on under my very nose."

"Quite ready?"

"That's what he said, and I thought the ruse was for *me*. Are you now in on his ill-treatment of me?"

"Della," Madeline said, "I have no intention of ever marrying the earl. It simply would not do."

"Why not?"

"What? I do not love him. He is in love with you." She stated this emphatically. "Whether he's aware of the fact, or not. As soon as Francesca arrives, we will move rapidly along with the plan."

"So I should hope," Della said, and sailed from the room.

Madeline shook her head. From spoiled child to countess in mere minutes. She did not envy the person who truly crossed Della Esmere.

Once Francesca arrived, Della definitely had other notions on her mind. Madeline persuaded her to cease her chatter until Francesca could have a wash and a nap. Then Madeline called for the Rowe carriage and they rode over to Hampden Hall. Much to the delight of Lady Hampden and her guests, the earl was absent and dinner was a solitary feminine affair, no holds drawn concerning the upper ten thousand. Tidbits of gossip reigned supreme.

At last at midnight when Della had gone to her room, Madeline faced Francesca's questioning countenance as they sat before the cold grate in the large guest bedchamber. "What has happened since our last letter?"

Smiling, Madeline said, "I have tried putting some gumption in her backbone, and at first it worked like a charm, yet lately, my good intentions of hoping Jaimie would see her as the one for him are all but vanished. Della found one day that she could order him about. I'm afraid she might harp like a shrew when they are alone."

Francesca shook her head. "A mistake indeed. Gentlemen do not take to bossing."

"She is not completely convinced that I have no interest in the earl, either."

"Yet she has gone along with your scheme to jolt him into awareness?"

Madeline hesitated, then nodded.

"Is it working?"

"She has such an impetuous nature that at times she takes two steps backward when she could be marching on ahead. I honestly do not know how to appraise what we have accomplished so far." Madeline kicked off her satin slippers and tucked her feet beneath her on the soft couch where she sat. "And since he has shown such blatant interest in me and other ladies in the neighborhood, she considers his attentions beneath her. She studies him, as I am sure she never has before, and I'm afraid she has found him lacking in some respects."

Francesca laughed. "Her infatuation has been diluted somewhat?"

"She considers him a fickle creature."

"Is there no competition for the earl? No other beaux for Della? What about the young gentlemen guests at this party she spoke of at dinner?"

"They adore her and sprinkle compliments, but I would call them boys."

Francesca chuckled and propped her feet on the striped ottoman that matched the upholstered furniture and curtains. "You are too wise for your own good."

"I'm not fond of this matchmaking chore, but I have observed them together enough to believe they do care a great deal about each other." She sighed.

"And the two families wish that they wed."

"Above all things they expect to join the two estates, but I don't know the exact wishes of my uncle and aunt."

Francesca nodded without comment, as though she knew there was more.

"I've spoken to Jaimie and told him I cannot marry him, and Uncle Bradford has agreed he will say nothing more of the proposed alliance between us."

"Then the field is clear. Does Della know this?"

"Yes, except she doesn't know that I spoke with her father, and I have this terrible sense that something I cannot control is hovering."

"Never fear. You have help now, and we shall press forward."

In the silence that followed, Francesca said, "Now that is settled, I have been dying to ask. . . . From all you have written me, I could not help noticing that Captain Titus Rhodes takes up a good deal of your thinking. In the beginning he was merely the captain, and now he is referred to as Titus. Is he very attentive, my dear?"

Madeline was appalled that she had been so transparent in her letters. "I should say no more so than to anyone else." From Francesca's knowing look she realized she was not fooling her with so weak an answer. Even though Francesca's interest seemed sincere, Madeline could not speak of him for fear the mere mention of his name on her lips would bring forth a surge of emotions.

A sharp tap at the door was accompanied by Della's raucous call. "Madeline, are you in there?"

Madeline groaned as Francesca answered, "Come in, Della."

With a sheepish grin, Della whisked into the room. "I heard your voices and I could not stay away."

Madeline sat up, crossing her feet at the ankles and patting the cushion beside her.

Della plopped down and nothing would do but for her to question Francesca about Madeline's London doings. It was obvious she was beside herself with such a notable visitor as Lady Francesca Rowe.

As graciously as a tired traveler could, Francesca assured Della that everything Madeline had told her about the shopping excursions on Bond Street, and the sights she had seen in London, was indeed the truth.

She informed them she planned to sleep until noon the following day. "I must set aside one day for making duty calls to some of my former neighbors, but what do you ladies have scheduled for our evening entertainment this week?"

Yawning, Madeline said, "Nothing definite, other than the assembly on Friday evening at the local hall in the village."

"Oh?"

Pouting, Della claimed, "Priscilla Milson is gloating to show off her town friends to the locals. She made sure her party would fall during the time of the only assembly of the summer."

Francesca smiled. "Ah, and you definitely do not care for this young lady."

Madeline cleared her throat. "Priscilla Milson chases dreadfully after the earl—"

"She always has," Della declared, "and Jaimie has never paid her any mind until this summer. He probably thinks I shall be hanging round waiting for him, and all he needs do is come fetch me." She crossed her arms over her bosom. "Well, I shall show him."

Madeline exchanged a furtive glance with Francesca, who then suggested that Della come to London and spend the little season at her home in Mayfair. "You are the age of most young ladies who have been on the town for at least a year or two, and you shall surely throw the London gentlemen into the boughs with your beauty."

"Oh! Thank you for the compliment." Della grabbed Madeline's elbow. "What do you think, Maddie?"

"Listen to Francesca, of course. We could bandy it about at the assembly that a trip to London is forthcoming."

Haughtily, Della said, "A trip to London for the small season."

"What an item to drop at the assembly," Madeline offered.

"Mama has been persuading Papa for months to go for the season, the real one, but I doubt she meant to include me."

Francesca looked vexed at this confession. "You must come next month, in September," she said, "and Madeline, too. We could have a marvelous time together."

"Thank you. I am most happy to accept your kind invitation. I'll write to Mama and Papa and tell them of our plans before their return."

"Perhaps the news of your intention to travel to London might set a fire under a certain local buck," Madeline teased.

Della took the opportunity to twit Madeline about the captain showing his face so often. "When he first returned from the military, he never accepted invitations," she told Francesca, "but now that Madeline is amongst us, he appears every-where."

"Titus no longer resides at Hampden Hall, true?" Francesca asked. "I believe he has bought the old Hollingsford home at the edge of Leaside."

While Madeline searched her mind for a less volatile subject to discuss, Della continued, "The captain's house is by far the grandest in the village, near eight bedrooms, all closed up of course. He and his manservant live there, but he hires women from Leaside who assist in the housekeeping and cooking."

"We must pay a neighborly call on him. It is my duty, you know, as he and his mother invited me here."

Recalling Almira's declaration that the captain never received visitors, Madeline stole a glance at Della, who looked as though she would burst into laughter any second. To forestall more talk of Captain Rhodes, she said, "The first thing we must do is to hire Pixie away from Hampden Hall. My abigail has been dressing Della, with Pixie's help here and there, but Pixie must be trained, for Della will need her own maid if she is to visit you in London."

Francesca appeared taken aback. "You speak as though you are planning to remain behind."

Madeline pulled the shawl from around her shoulders and spread it across her knees. "We shall see."

"Pixie is an abigail, I assume?"

"At present she is a maid in the earl's service, but devoted to Della. I could train her myself, but I doubt I would have the time."

"*You*, Maddie?" Della asked with obvious doubt of Madeline's ability in her voice.

"Yes. I braid, twist, curl, and with the correct herbs, I can color hair." She stood and, placing her hand on the back of the couch, told them about Esther. "She is British, of course, twelve years older than I, and one of the constant household servants my family employed. I was raised as any young British girl would have been, had my family remained in England after my birth, except that I have had some unique experiences unheard of in this country." She paused to draw a quick breath. "My mother's Irish maid, who died of the same disease as Mama, personally trained Esther. I followed Esther's every step, so I, as well, absorbed the lessons."

Madeline glanced at Della, who was staring at her in awed silence.

"What an adventurous life you have led, Maddie," Della offered.

"And having this training allows you the knowledge of whether or not an abigail knows her business," Francesca said. "I do so admire you."

"But the restraint I hear in your voice tells me I should allow her to do the training."

"Esther should perform the service. You are no longer in Canada."

"True. And how much more complicated my life has become."

In the carriage the next afternoon, Madeline noted the twinkle in Francesca's eyes when she said, "My husband's nephew, Abel Fredricks, will pay me a visit soon. He travels round the racing circuit with a distant cousin of mine, Vincent Brock. They will most likely stay at the Green Dragon and should arrive before the start of the local races at Farringdon Downs." She smiled at Della. "I am counting on their appearance on the scene to lend some spice to the neighborhood gatherings."

Madeline had met the nephew during her stay in London; she nodded at Francesca's unspoken question. Mr. Fredricks would do very well as competition for the earl. A polished Corinthian, he was both handsome and elegant. "Let us hope the gentlemen make it here before the assembly." Some attention to Della by truly sophisticated gentlemen, and certainly one as fashionable as Francesca's nephew, should rouse Jaimie's jealousy. For a certainty.

Francesca leaned across and patted Della's hand.

Madeline continued, "Nothing makes a lady more appealing to a gentleman than when he sees other males bestowing her with attention and compliments."

With a determined light in her eyes, Francesca said, "Yes, and Abel owes me a few favors. Besides, I control his allowance."

From what she had seen of Abel Fredricks, Madeline doubted he would need a bribe. He was as full of himself as were Jaimie and Nicholas Wardton.

They made three duty calls, and Francesca spoke frankly to Della on the way back to Esmere Grange. "Madeline tells me some of the young gentlemen of the village and round about often call on you at the Grange."

"Since Madeline has come to live with us."

Both Madeline and Francesca ignored the petulant comment.

"Should any call at a later date," Francesca continued, "especially the earl, no matter what time he arrives, you must keep him waiting."

Della nodded. "Shall I offer him tea?"

"Tea? Heavens no." Francesca's face was a study at such a naive suggestion.

Madeline smiled and whispered, "If it is morning, do not offer him anything, for he may only stay a short while. If it is afternoon, offer him a glass of wine."

Della's gasp was proof she thought this whole two weeks a great adventure. "I am so glad you have come to visit us, Lady Rowe. Aren't you, Madeline? We would never be allowed this freedom with my mama around."

Madeline laughed outright, and Francesca said, "La, child, you are a delight."

Della had always been treated as a child and now suddenly was thrust into the role of a young lady. Heady circumstances indeed, Madeline thought.

Dusk fell as Titus reined his gray over the stream at the footbridge on Esmere property. He skirted the gardens and whistled for a boy as he drew up to the stable yard. He decided he should have allowed Bradford to cancel the trip to Bath when Bradford realized the three women would be at Esmere Grange without a male protector. He had had to assure Bradford he would visit often, placing the neighbors on notice that a gentleman would be around if trouble arose.

Waste of energy, he grumbled. There were the male servants, the stable lot, and shepherds. Rough and tumble men, the shepherds. He had not thought his promise would make him a surrogate father to Della.

He handed over his reins to an elderly and bent stableman, and walked around the house, coming up short at the sight of two lads holding the horse of a smart cabriolet out front.

Damn. That meant there were visitors, and probably from London, judging by the looks of the rig. He tried to convince himself his resentment toward this vehicle with its shiny black paint edged with ornamental gilding had nothing to do with the fact that it was sparkling new, while his own curricle, dusty and white with mildew, sat idle in the Hollingsford coach house.

His mood grew fouler by the minute. All he had wanted was a few moments alone with Madeline concerning Jaimie's and Della's romance. Their best laid plans, contrived without the other's knowledge, were in danger of going awry, and he was the culprit intending to tear them asunder.

He was not dressed for calling on ladies. Scowling down at his riding jacket and buckskins, he dusted his gloves and marched to the front door. Positive the guests were more than likely male, he would just make some subtle effort to discover their intentions.

In the drawing room, ensconced comfortably in chairs before the summer screens of the cold fireplace, were Vincent Brock and Abel Fredricks. This put him in a vile humor indeed. He considered both men a threat to his peace of mind.

He had met the nephew during his recuperation at Francesca's home. In that short span of time he'd learned three things about him: besides his dark good looks, he was worse than a hanger-on, devilishly appealing to the ladies, and full of his own consequence.

Vincent Brock he had not seen in years. What he remembered of him bordered on the criminal: he favored female children. He wondered if his fancy now ran to young ladies? Although Titus knew Brock was not a man of means, his smart tailoring set him apart, and he wore his gray hair with style.

Why was Francesca racketing about with them, and how dare she bring them here amongst such nubile ladies?

11

As soon as he had stepped across the threshold, Madeline came forward, and was now saying, "Why, Captain Rhodes, you are scowling as though you have met with misfortune. Do come in and rest."

Della chimed in with "Have you been robbed, Captain?" her voice full of amusement.

However, the gentlemen lounging in the comfortable chairs did not mistake his frown. Looking pointedly at them, Titus gave a cursory bow, coupled with a curt "Good evening."

They immediately took the hint, said their farewells, and withdrew, but not before arranging to meet the ladies next day.

When he heard the horse head out, Titus said to Francesca, "If Fredricks is running with Brock nowadays, you can expect demands of extensions on his allowance." He settled into the deep chair opposite Madeline, and prepared to stay until he had some answers.

Francesca merely smiled. "An extraordinary greeting, Titus, I must say."

"Is that what they call rudeness in England? Extraordinary?" The consternation in Madeline's eyes and voice made him pause.

"Yes, you have caught me out." He included all three ladies in his gaze. "Please allow me to apologize for my abrupt and unforgivable discourtesy. I fear my weariness has control of my tongue."

"Say no more," Francesca said, "but what has made you so frazzled?"

"I've been the day at Hollingsford Farm, walking the hedges and inspecting the buildings."

"Hollingsford land is the neighboring farm the other side of Hampden," Della said in explanation to Madeline and Francesca. "It has been up for sale nearly five years."

Titus smiled at Della. "I have purchased it. I mean to lease the land to tenants for the time being." He did not mention in this elegant drawing room that he might possibly offer it as the future site of a small factory. That he should contemplate going into trade would shock Francesca and Della, to be sure. But the lady whose opinion he cared for was Madeline. Somehow he felt her practical mind would welcome his decision as worthwhile business for a man.

For a man who had barely missed the death rider on the battlefield and who had experienced the world through stark and uncolored glass. She, too, had seen the world in a similar way.

"How exciting, Captain," Madeline said. "Are you going to live there and be our close neighbor? What of your home in the village?"

"Whoa, I have only just bought the land, and plans are still undecided. As for my house . . . No, I do not expect I shall move. I like my establishment very much, thank you."

"What business sense you have developed, Titus. I wish Rowe could have seen it."

"I cannot help but feel Rowe would be somewhat concerned for his nephew. Why is it Fredricks does not wear the British uniform? He appears able-bodied."

"There is an elderly uncle with influence."

Titus snorted at her explanation.

"Really, Titus, Abel is quite safe. Brock is my distant cousin and an eager escort when I need one. I should be insulted if you were not such an old friend."

Titus sloughed off her remark as absurdity. "You are in great demand, never in need of a cousin for an escort. Vincent Brock has to be twenty years older than you."

He noted that she threw Madeline an amused glance before answering. "Now that you mention it, he is a very, very distant cousin, and his age is the same as mine, Titus. Two and thirty, a year younger than yourself."

"He looks half a century. Must be the gallivanting around the country with that disreputable set of his."

"Did not you and Bradford once run with the same set?" Francesca asked.

"That was before I went to Spain."

Madeline rose from the straight-backed chair and walked slowly to the sandalwood buffet where she poured sherry into a glass. "When I was in London visiting Francesca, before coming to Leaside, I had the pleasure of meeting Mr. Abel Fredricks. I found him an attentive gentleman. And Mr. Brock was all politeness to me." She brought the glass to him. "You have spent too many hours in the saddle and on foot, and you needn't think you must ride over to Esmere to check on us."

Thanking her for the drink, he swallowed it in one gulp, both pleased and irritated that she had read him so easily. "Nonsense, Bradford has left me in charge is all."

"I was led to believe that I, as chaperon, was in charge of the young ladies," Francesca said with a grin.

"I see what it is, Francesca," Madeline put in, staring a challenge at him. "He is our designated male protector and all that."

The ladies laughed and Titus resisted the urge to ask Madeline if she had slept well the previous night. He did not have to change the topic of conversation, for Della did it for him.

"Just think, Captain, I am to go to Lady Rowe's home in London for the little season. She has invited me, and Madeline, of course."

This news hit him like a heavy fire of artillery. Madeline was up to everything, but she did not know her way against the scheming minds of men such as Abel Fredricks, or Vincent Brock. If she goes to London with Della, they will eat her alive. He would have to go with them.

Madeline had not slept at all. She still could not believe what she had witnessed in the drawing room just last night. Captain Rhodes, Titus, was sweet on Francesca.

Was that the real reason he had invited Francesca to Leaside? His scowling presence and criticism of Mr. Brock was blatant concern for Francesca and her cousin's obvious pursuit. The captain probably realized the relationship of kin did not matter. Distant cousins often wed.

And what of his attentiveness toward her? Had it been meaningless to him? She saw now she had been nothing but a diversion for him. She made a silent pledge to bring her emotions under control.

She could not compete with such a diamond as Francesca. Nor would she wish to. Francesca had been too kind to her. How humiliating that she should be attracted to a man, who in turn, desired her dear friend.

At first sight she had been intuitive of him. He was indeed a pirate, a brigand, and she would eat his black heart before leaving this place.

They were in Aunt Almira's dressing room; Madeline, Della, Francesca, Esther, and now Pixie. Over at Hampden Hall, Lady Hampden was this minute arranging for Pixie to move into Esmere Grange.

The large room, paneled with mahogany wardrobes, housed a long dressing table lined with jars of creams, bottled glass containers, and silver brushes. A mirror stood on a swivel stand near the lone window. To the right of the door was a long, tall table used for pressing clothes. Looking at Esther, Madeline said, "You will need a small stove for heating the irons."

Esther nodded and left the room.

Francesca sat on the dressing table stool, allowing Madeline full charge, as it had been her idea.

In brisk words, Madeline informed the young maid, Pixie, of her duties. "You are in the service of Lord Esmere now, and an understudy to Esther, who will mold you into an abigail. When she has finished with you, Lady Rowe and I will expect you to be an exact replica of what a lady wishes when she hires a maid to look after her."

The maid stood in the middle of the room, staring at Madeline.

"There is no time to waste, Pixie, now you are here. You must move your belongings into the Grange. There can be no more hopping back and forth between the two houses."

Madeline could not understand why the maid looked at her with such puzzlement. Perhaps it was because she had always been so friendly before, and now was speaking as though she, Madeline, were her mistress. "You have much to learn in a very short space if you wish to become a proper lady's maid," Madeline said when Pixie did not move.

Exasperated, Madeline stared at the maid, frowning. "Hop to it, girl. You've work to do."

Coming to life at last, Pixie bobbed. "Right away, Miss." She fled the room, her cap ribbons flaring out behind her.

"Ah, the Canadian miss speaks sharply, does she?" Francesca said. "I doubt that young one has ever had such an earnest scold."

Della shrugged. "It is not the first time Madeline has bullied us around here."

Laughing, Francesca clapped her hands. "I am happy to hear it, for the man I have in mind for our Canadian miss would not stand for a lady who bowed and asked him his every wish." She gazed at Madeline. "It's likely he would admire this commanding streak you have."

Madeline's hands went to her cheeks. She regretted her outburst against poor Pixie. It was from her lack of sleep, but more from her anger at the captain. "No more matchmaking, please. My nerves are worn thin."

Madeline watched the gentlemen crowding each other in the hall at the foot of the stairs at Esmere Grange. Sparkling white cravats competed with embroidered waist coats as the earl and Nicholas Wardton, along with Fredricks and Brock, waited for Della.

Since his visit several nights ago, Captain Rhodes had been noticeably absent during the rest of the week. Madeline wondered if he would be at the assembly.

She had left Della alone with Esther and Pixie, and had joined Francesca to greet their escorts. Too many escorts for only three ladies, but they had deliberately planned it this way for Jaimie's benefit. "Let him see her in the midst of admiring gentlemen," Madeline had told Francesca.

The boards at the top of the stairs creaked, and there, in a rustle of skirts, was Della, taking the steps sedately and looking radiant. Barely a trace of plumpness remained, and Madeline thought she had never seen her more beautiful. Only someone with her dark hair and ivory skin could wear the pale yellow gown and have it enhance her appearance. It did indeed set off the strand of pearls with its single pear-shaped diamond.

The gentlemen stood in stunned silence as Della moved slowly toward them. "Why, Madeline . . . Lady Rowe, are all these gentlemen waiting for us?"

"My, my," Mr. Brock said. "Such a princess."

Madeline regretted her scheming when Abel Fredricks stepped up and met Della on the fourth step from the bottom. He looked like a man with stars in his eyes. Francesca had talked to him, requesting he show Della special attention. But from where Madeline stood, she thought Mr. Fredricks was putting it on a bit too heavily.

"Allow me," he said as he took Della's hand, placed it on his arm, and walked with her down to the tiled floor.

Madeline stole a glance at Francesca, who whispered, "Do not worry so. He knows what he is about."

"But does Della?" Madeline murmured. Her cousin's starry-eyed gaze looked genuine. Madeline groaned. What she needed were some headache powders.

Jaimie had called, expecting to escort Della to the assembly, but he, too, watched immobile and speechless as Fredricks placed Della's cape around her shoulders and they glided out together to Francesca's carriage, Francesca and her cousin, Mr. Brock, trailing behind.

At the end of this dreamlike scene, Madeline left the house with a subdued Jaimie on one arm, and Nicky Wardton on the other. Silence descended on the trio inside the Hampden carriage, and stubbornly, she refused to resort to chit-chat.

When Titus was younger he had thought better of Leaside's assembly hall than this. It was barely more than a warehouse, its walls and floor crammed with every local in the territory, and too noisy by far. Young and old joked and laughed with one another above the racket of the band of four players. The music, if one could call it that, grew louder with each tune, while the laced punch flowed in abundance, and mixed with the whiskey, rum, and ale, created a merry crowd indeed.

Jaimie was on one side of Titus, Wardton on the other, and both of them gabbing at once. They were standing on the sidelines watching the dancing.

Wardton jabbered on, gesturing with his hands. Titus nodded occasionally, but really had no idea what the conversation was about. Instead, he watched Madeline dancing the steps of a country jig with Abel Fredricks. She had not graced a chair since her arrival, and from Francesca's behavior tonight, one would never know she was a town-polished dame.

He narrowed his eyes as he observed Fredricks. He had arrived at the assembly with Della on his arm, and when he danced with her, he appeared smooth, practiced, and plain to see, artificial. But now with Madeline, the adoration in his eyes seemed real. For certain the seasoned young gent knew how to charm a lady. He had upstaged Jaimie and stolen Della from under his nose. How successful would he be with Madeline?

Titus's head ached and his leg pained him something terrible, rendering him more tense by the minute. It was high time he suggest to Jaimie that they escort the ladies back to Esmere before this wild state of confusion turned into a debacle. It was as though every living mortal here sought revelry in the hopes of warding off the autumn and winter.

He went swiftly across the floor to the small stage where the band played and, slipping the violinist a shilling, asked if the next tune would be a waltz. The rotund man informed him, "We play only one waltz, sir, as we have the music for no others, and we had planned it for the last dance of the evening."

Titus clunked down three more shillings, demanding, "A waltz, now if you please."

The violinist nodded assent, swept up the money, and announced the band would take a short break, wherein all four members headed straight for the improvised tavern. He bowed as he passed Titus. "Your request in a matter of minutes, sir."

Later in the evening, Jaimie approached Madeline and Francesca, saying he wished to offer for Della and declare his intentions to Lord Esmere. "I don't know whether I should ride down to Bath or wait for his return."

Madeline stared at him for a minute, then said, "Wait, by all means. Allow the man his holiday." At last, what she had hoped for—Jaimie offering for Della. *If only Della will behave sensibly.*

Della was off dancing with Francesca's nephew and heard nothing of this, and later Madeline could not tell if Jaimie had indeed spoken to her, for Della laughed and talked with everyone and did not mention Jaimie's name.

Madeline smiled and danced with everyone who asked her. She kept telling herself what a good time she was having, but the face of Captain Rhodes loomed everywhere, even when he was not within sight. And then suddenly he was right beside her.

The band played a waltz and while she unconsciously went through the steps with him, her mind ran rampant. *How could he look at her with such intensity if he was in love with someone else? How dare he influence her brain and body alike.* Shivers chased up and down her spine while she told her mind to shut up. *Enjoy what moments you have with him, for soon you shall leave, and start a new life, and . . .*

Titus laughed inwardly. For the first time during the evening he was truly enjoying himself. Each time he came near Madeline he could feel her sparks seducing him. Merely holding her while dancing was enchantment. She was a witch and he a willing victim.

He remembered their kiss, remembered the honey taste of her lips, recalling with renewed pleasure that she had responded with abandon. Of that he was certain.

After the waltz he held on to her wrist and she had no choice but to follow him. She laughed outright at the stares some of the matrons threw their way, and Titus thought how much he admired that unperturbed trait in her. She never hid her smiles behind a fan, and when she laughed it was a clear and joyful sound, causing a surge of emotions inside him, only one of which was happiness.

He set his lips in a determined smile while he searched the crowd for Della and Francesca. "Jaimie and I will see you ladies home," he said when he found them having a glass of lemonade with Fredricks and Brock.

"That is not necessary," Madeline retorted. "We can manage quite well, thank you."

He noticed that the gentlemen did not object to his suggestion. He lingered, studying Madeline's face to see if there was genuine reluctance to end the evening with him. His loyal friend, Francesca, came to his rescue.

"Thank you so much, Titus, I have a fearful headache." She turned to Madeline. "I assure you, I am more than ready for my bed." She instructed Brock to see her carriage was delivered to the house.

Titus was relieved, for he and Jaimie had set up their plans together. Besides which, Titus had brought his curricle for the express purpose of seeing Madeline home. He bowed and gestured for Jaimie, who called for the Hampden carriage.

Titus escorted Madeline outside and took a direct route back to Esmere Grange, not bothering to wait for the others. He had not had a chance to speak with her about the romance between Della and Jaimie, yet he hardly knew where to begin. "We must talk."

"Very well."

He could feel her gaze on him in the dark night. "I know how you have worked to ally Jaimie and Della, and I appreciate your efforts."

Her sigh was audible. "This sounds as though you are about to tell me something I might not wish to hear."

"Maybe they are too young to wed."

"You can suggest they are too young? I thought you were all for the alliance. What has happened to the attempt to save the Hampden estate?"

"Something new has developed. Quite possibly we could receive an exorbitant sum of money soon. If so, the marriage will not be necessary."

"How mercenary you sound, as though Jaimie and Della could be offered up like the pigs at market." She moved as far from him as was possible on the narrow seat. "It's too late. You should have thought of this earlier in the game."

Driving these country roads at night required great concentration, and Titus dared not turn his attention away from his horses to face her. "I regret any misdirection I, or Jaimie, may have presented."

"You regret? I wipe my hands of the whole affair, Captain Rhodes, and I wish you good luck in your new venture to save the estate. Whatever it may be." They had arrived at the Grange, and she climbed down before he had time to come around to assist her.

He whistled for the stableboys and followed her inside as she continued with "And I hope your plan does not burst into pieces in your face."

In the drawing room, he fidgeted like some youngster, certain he would lose this battle. "You have to admit they both are changed in their behavior."

"But not in their feelings toward one another."

He tightened his jaw. "Della has established her place as the local beauty."

"And Jaimie has finally seen her in that light." She paused as though there was more to say.

"What is it? What are you leaving unsaid?"

"She truly wants this trip to London, and I think if she meets with too much adversity from her mother, she may just pick up her skirts and walk out."

"That independent is she?"

"Yes, she has an inbred confidence, and now that she knows men find her attractive and enjoy her company, no one will hold her back." She gestured toward a chair, but since she did not sit, neither did Titus. "She and Francesca have been over the whole house, inspecting the linen chests, the silver, even the wine bottles."

"I won't ask the stupid question of 'what on earth for?' I assume this is tutoring for running a household? Even if one has a loyal butler, there is much the lady of the house must oversee."

She nodded. "Francesca instructs her as to when and if the linens are to be replaced, why counting the silver is important, even, as you say, if the butler can be trusted. Many guests come into a huge house such as Hampden Hall, and things have a way of disappearing, she says, so the mistress must be on her toes and know whom to invite back and whom to exclude."

They heard the horses and the squeaking of Jaimie's carriage then, and both sat down simultaneously on opposite ends of the sofa.

Titus was surprised when Jaimie did not come in with Della and Francesca. "Where is Jaimie?"

Della, with a mulish look on her face, plopped down in a deep chair. "I did not invite him in."

Titus glanced at Madeline. He had followed her into the house as a matter of course, assuming he was welcome.

"Why did we have to leave so early?" Della demanded of Madeline. "Just when I was having a wonderful time."

Titus caught Madeline's quick look in his direction that clearly stated, *It was not my decision,* but aloud she said, "Francesca has the headache."

At mention of her, Francesca went straight through to the buffet and poured herself some wine, offering the decanter to them also. No one accepted.

Titus supposed from Della's petulant behavior that some heated words must have been exchanged in the carriage. When he glanced back at Madeline, she gave him a smug smile and lowered her eyelids as though hiding some triumph. A cautious chill crept into his bones. He had seen that look before and it meant trouble.

"What do you think, Della?" Madeline uttered in a low, soft voice. "A romantic evening you have had this night."

Della agreed with a simpering smile. "Abel Fredricks is a dashing gentleman."

"Indeed he is, but I was speaking of Jaimie. Are you excited?"

"About what?"

Francesca walked over to the sofa then and sat down between them. They were all facing Della.

"Did he ask you anything of importance?" Madeline asked.

Della gave her characteristic shrug. "He asked me only for a dance." She looked from one lady to the other. "Why are you both staring like that? What? What is it?"

Madeline laughed lightly. "Only that he told us he wished to speak to Uncle Bradford and declare his intentions."

Della's eyes grew wide. "For truth?" The joy in her voice was evident, then quickly replaced with obstinacy. "I shall refuse him. He is not the only man who wants me."

Madeline shot up from the sofa, her scent of lemon verbena wafting from her green skirts. It struck Titus as fresh and enticing, as she was.

He rose and strolled over to the sandalwood buffet and leaned against it where he could observe all three ladies in this interesting turn of events. Madeline was indeed one jump ahead of him, as he had had no idea Jaimie was so close to an offer.

"Della, you must not behave so impulsively," Madeline pleaded. "Jaimie has such pride. If you refuse him, he might not ask again."

"I don't care."

"You *do* care."

"Does this have anything to do with why you were rude to him on the way home?" Francesca asked. "Good heavens, girl. You cannot mean to refuse him."

A dark red crept up Della's face and her eyes filled with tears. "If I should refuse him, I wouldn't be surprised if he ran straight to Priscilla's house and—" she hiccuped, "offered for her."

"You don't believe any such thing!" Madeline said.

Amused with the bickering, Titus interrupted, "Now see what happens when one meddles in the affairs of others," and immediately he realized his mistake. The last thing he should have directed toward Madeline was a chiding.

She turned on him, her hands balled into fists on her hips. "Do not worry, Captain. Before too long, I shall no longer be an interloper. Esther and I have discussed our future, and we shall soon be out of the way here."

"Nonsense."

"We expect to open a business on the outskirts of some small resort town, or in a trade community near London. We have much to offer in the training of young ladies, or their maids."

"You will do no such thing," he declared, appalled that she could think of leaving. "This is not Canada. We are a civilized country and expect our ladies to behave in a proper manner and do what is expected of them." He was barely conscious of Francesca quietly rising and urging Della from the room.

"How dare you think you have the right to tell me what I might do with my life. You do as you wish with your own, but you would have me strapped into the English mold? No, thank you, sir."

He tried to turn this ugly tide. He wanted to spar with her in their usual manner. "There, you see? You expect a man to put up with an impertinent female?"

"Am I?"

This was no fun anymore. "A serious argument is what you want? All right, I'll oblige. You are an impertinent woman, turning a sweet girl like Della into a—a—"

"A lady," Madeline supplied.

"She is as much like my spoiled little brother as possible."

"You cannot still be thinking of him as your *little* brother?"

Ignoring her snide remark, he wagged a finger under her nose. "Do not speak to me of how well Della will manage him as his countess, either, my girl. You are the manipulator here. He cares nothing for the farms, and crops, or the buildings. Talks incessantly of horses."

"Perhaps with time, as he learns the importance of those things?"

"See? You are at it even now." He continued, pacing and talking to himself, truly irritated. "And there's your influence on Grandma'am. My own grandmother, for whom I have made a fortune by investing her jointure—" He faced her. "Not to mention my mother. I had her ready to retire to country living, refurbished the Dower House, and now what does she announce? She and Grandma'am are contemplating a journey to London for the little season."

"Your mother is too young and lively to be stuffed away in a dower house."

It was true. Grudgingly, he admitted, "You are right on that score."

"Thank you," she said, and laughed derisively.

"What about Bradford, my own good friend. Boyhood friend I'll have you know. He's gone off half-cocked over a woman he's lived with for eighteen years!"

No comment, her face a bland mask.

"Because of you, I am actually looking at Almira in a different light. Softheaded is what I'd call it. Good God. That one miss from Canada could cause such havoc!"

"Are you finished?"

"No."

She crossed her arms over her high-waisted dress. "You have had far too much to drink."

"Not half as much as I plan."

She set her jaw, and he braced himself for a barrage of insults. Instead, in a swirl of green silk that matched her angry green eyes, she left him standing there in the drawing room.

During his speech, he had absentmindedly picked up one of Bradford's cigars, and now he threw it across the room, not caring where it landed.

In the corridor, Francesca waited for him. "You simpleton, Titus. Why are you dallying? Some Corinthian will steal her from under your nose if she spends any time at all in London."

He owed no one an explanation for his actions.

He turned and stalked out, slamming the door with a ringing crash that frightened his horses. The boys had to soothe them as they pranced for some yards before quieting enough for him to drive away.

12

Madeline sank back on the soft, lace-trimmed pillows of her bed. At last she was alone and could let down her guard. Strange how she wanted to cry, but no tears fell. She felt as though all her emotions had seeped out, leaving her insides cold and bare. She hunched her shoulders, pulling the bedcovers to her chin. She had come here longing for a place to call her own, and thought she'd found her refuge at Leaside, a natural haven. But she had not been prepared for love.

Ah, that last was a lie. After meeting Captain Titus Rhodes she'd known he was a man who could fill her whole life with love.

Somehow she managed to sleep, and awoke the next morning to another beautiful, sunny day. Here were more long hours ahead of her. Why couldn't it rain for heaven's sake! Then she would have an excuse to stay in her room, and not have to laugh and smile and listen to twitting chitchat.

It was the week of the Farringdon Downs Races. The Leaside villagers and their neighbors had waited all year for this particular event, and Madeline, Della, and Francesca were invited to grand parties.

Francesca remembered attending the races when she had been a child. "But it was nothing like this," she said. "It has grown into a regular social season."

"This will be my first meet since I was ten," Della said, beside herself with excitement.

It was customary for ladies to watch the races from the safety of open carriages. They sat with their parasols at the ready while gentlemen strolled from barouches to various gigs, tipping their hats and complimenting each damsel. In addition, the Esmere group had hit on a daily ritual: luncheon every day before the races; dinner and dancing afterward at numerous country homes. Each time they visited Hampden Hall, they met more fashionable racegoers housed there.

"No doubt if Aunt Almira and Uncle Bradford were at home, they too would be sending out invitations to parties at the Grange," Madeline murmured.

"Oh, yes," Della replied. "This is the time of year when no one is a stranger."

Ordinarily, Madeline would have loved all the festivities, but she simply could not enter into the spirit of things. The antagonism and resentment directed toward Captain Rhodes would not go away. She felt more like an interloper than ever. In the early morning hours, and in the evenings when she dressed for dinner, she discussed with Esther where they should go.

And when.

Madeline spent a good part of the week deflecting Jaimie's indignation. She talked long and hard, trying to convince him that Della was testing his emotions and that he must not rush his fences; he must wait until Saturday to declare himself when Uncle Bradford was expected to return from Bath. She urged him to behave nonchalantly toward his rival. "The more you resist his presence in squiring her, the more determined Della will become in ignoring *you*."

Still, at every opportunity, Jaimie cut Fredricks dead, leaving in a huff on several occasions.

Reluctantly, he had rejoined their excursions, and now Madeline regretted her interference from the beginning. She was sick of soothing Jaimie's resentful attitude, and tired of his declarations of undying devotion to her while he pined like a puppy after Della. Equally sick of Abel Fredricks throwing her wicked glances while whispering in Della's ear. She feared things were fast running out of hand.

Fredricks had bewitched Della. The man *was* handsome, though in a cold, hard way, with nothing soft or gentle in his smile.

And then there was Nicholas Wardton back in their midst, hovering at their elbows. Although he often managed to stroll with Della into the nearby thickets, Madeline did not think he would go beyond gentlemanly bounds. Yet, she was convinced he did nothing without a self-serving reason.

She supposed it was natural for Francesca to pair herself with her cousin, Mr. Brock. That way, if the captain joined the party, Francesca could feel free to flirt with him. After all, cousins were dispensable.

As the carriage neared the Downs, Madeline noted that for some unknown reason, Della was in an ill humor. "Out of sorts, are we?" Madeline teased. "Are your suitors arguing again?"

"My suitors, indeed. Jaimie spends more time with you than me."

"Give him half a chance, and he shall stick to your side." Madeline's patience was stretched to snapping.

Francesca gave Della a smart tap on the wrist with her fan. "You should not have worn your pearls."

Della fingered the necklace. "I receive such compliments when I wear them."

"If the necklace is lost," Madeline said, "we shall never find it in this mob." She restrained an impulse to yank the matching earrings from her cousin's ears.

Even before Madeline stepped from the carriage, she was aware that on this, the last day of the races, Captain Rhodes stood with the usual array of gentlemen. She had the uncanny impression he waited for her. It was the presence of expectancy he presented, his tall figure dressed in blue superfine, his immaculate buckskins tucked into the military-style boots he wore. He was not dressed for inspecting farmland this day.

All up and down the thoroughfare the scene was the same. Gentlemen lounged beside their ladies, munching sandwiches and fruit, spilling as much liquor as they swallowed. The ladies' skirts spread out around them sprinkled a spectrum of hues across the green grass, from pale primrose and sweet pinks to rich iris purple. The gentlemen's darker jackets framed the painting, their vests of floral themes adding a lively twist.

Titus came forward, bowed, and addressed her formally. "Miss Smythe?"

"Yes?" she answered, frowning up into those stormy eyes.

He drummed his fingers on his hat brim, scrutinizing her. With such a look, she experienced a hot tide of embarrassment. Was he comparing her simple gown of sprigged muslin with its square-cut neckline to Francesca's Paris creation of crisp black on white stripes?

His brows meeting, he asked if she would accompany him to the meat pie vendors.

"La, Captain," Francesca put in, "but we have food aplenty. Why do you not join us?" She waved a hand at two footmen from the Grange who were arranging cloths and cushions on the ground.

"Underneath the shade of that oak tree's mighty branches, Captain, you might regain your good humor," Madeline said, and waited for his answer.

Della giggled and Fredricks smirked as Francesca led them away to the picnic.

There was a shout and they both turned to see Jaimie waving. "Do hurry," he urged. "We are famished."

The captain walked toward the picnicking couples with Madeline and they kept up a steady flow of polite comments. She wanted to race right to the point, to the heart of the relationship between them, assuming there was one. If she broached the subject and was rejected . . . could she graciously bluff her way out of the situation? She thought not.

While they were out of earshot of the others, she slowed down. "I am afraid I was quite rude to you after the assembly. I wish to apologize for showing such obstinate behavior to someone who has been more than kind to me during my stay here." She chose polite words, hoping her attitude toward him came across as indifferent.

He stopped and took her hand from his arm, facing her. "I'm the one who should apologize. I have to admit I admire your ambition. To venture on your own, with only your maid, takes courage, even from a lady who has been in the midst of battles."

Madeline could not have been more shocked. But then, this change of attitude proved that he really did not care if she stayed, or went. She had her answer.

They walked on and she studied his profile as he looked in Francesca's direction. She was sitting with Titus's mother and Grandma'am in their open barouche pulled under the trees. Della, Fredricks, and Mr. Brock stood beside the carriage, and from a distance, it appeared that Fredricks and Mr. Brock were entertaining the lot of them with some humorous story.

Everything on the captain's face closed up and he said, "I regret Francesca's choice of male companions."

It seemed as if the sun searched out Madeline, burning through her bonnet. Anger and disappointment rushed through her, for here was more proof that he cared for Francesca. She worried not one whit whether she hid her feelings, but aloud she merely said, "It is a beautiful day for an outing."

She swallowed hard as his gaze bored into hers. Then, he glanced at the distant clouds. "We'll have rain before dusk."

Even though the captain stayed with their party, he kept a polite distance from her, and she thought it strange he did not seek out Francesca's company.

The afternoon dragged on; Madeline had no appetite for the basket treats the Esmere cook had provided, or for the races.

The carriages, filled now with onlookers for the final runs, lined up side by side. Madeline searched for Della, then noticed she was sitting beside Mr. Brock in his cabriolet. The captain and Jaimie lounged close by, ignoring Mr. Wardton, who hovered near the rig. They were probably discussing their wagers again. She had heard nothing else for most of the day.

She saw Mr. Wardton climb onto Brock's smart vehicle and sit on the groom's support positioned at the rear and between the wheels. She thought it odd, but assumed he had chosen that spot for viewing the next race.

She intended to join Francesca and Grandma'am in Lady Hampden's barouche when Mr. Fredricks strolled over to her and asked a question.

"I beg your pardon," she said to his frowning face, "but what were you saying?"

Fredricks repeated his question in regard to the dancing party to be held that evening.

"I wish to skip the party altogether." Then, thinking how rude her reply sounded, she added, "Please forgive my abruptness, but the sun has given me a headache."

Fredricks bowed and asked if she would care to stroll across the way. He gestured toward the cabriolet. "Mr. Brock will relinquish his seat for such a lovely lady."

She meant to refuse but hit on the notion that if they were alone she could request he cease his amorous attentions directed at Della. She pushed up her parasol and walked along leisurely with him.

Titus knew if he stood there long enough, Fredricks would make his move. Jaimie had been right in his reporting, and Titus had tried not to reveal that he cared if Fredricks dangled after Miss Smythe for the whole week.

He watched Fredricks emerge from the picnic area where he had left Della sitting with Brock and Wardton. Fredricks then approached Madeline just as she was about to join the older ladies in their carriage.

Titus felt like a fool, waiting and spying like this. Why in hell hadn't he said what he meant in the first place? Like an idiot, he'd asked her to accompany him to the meat pie vendors. How gauche could one man be.

He tensed. Fredricks and Madeline were passing within a carriage space of him. He didn't catch what Fredricks had just said, but it must have concerned a losing wager, for Madeline looked as though she were commiserating with him.

As they turned in his direction, Madeline's voice carried clearly. "I am sorry to hear that. Such a rotten run of luck."

"Yes, we shall have to leave tomorrow."

Good riddance.

"The racing will be over here. Will you go on to a new track?"

Their voices trailed off.

No more indecision. He intended to speak his mind, and if Fredricks wanted to witness his blundering, so be it.

"I wonder if you would consider turning off the charm toward Della." Madeline took a long breath, feeling a momentary twinge of uncertainty, speaking to Fredricks in this way.

Fredricks had been humming off-key and stopped suddenly at her suggestion. "My dear, certainly, but what is the prize?"

She had been right about his smile. At this moment it was an outright leer. He stepped closer and the odor of wine on his breath overwhelmed her.

Looking back over his shoulder he said, "This is an indelicate situation, but what are you offering in exchange?"

Had she heard him correctly?

"I have never met anyone like you," Fredricks said, this time slurring his words.

How stupid of her to have been so preoccupied with herself that she had ignored his obvious intoxication. She glanced around and saw that Captain Rhodes was approaching. It would take him only moments to overcome them.

She swung back to Fredricks and found him waiting with an expectant look on his face. *Good heavens, did he actually expect a response?*

The incongruity of the situation, of her whole life, in fact, set her off in peals of laughter. Barely aware that the captain now stood beside her, she pointed a finger at Fredricks's astonished face. "You—you—"

Down the path came the owners and attending company, leading their prize blood horses to the turf. All sorts of hangers-on followed from the nearby stables, each intent on his own purpose, whether it be as servant or bookmaker.

Beyond the tents, the horse-mad English crowd parted for the impressive parade, and Fredricks disappeared amongst them. Still, Madeline could not control her giggles.

She sobered instantly when she looked up and saw Della unclasp her pearls and hold them out for Mr. Brock to inspect. She frowned into the sunshine. "Silly girl. What is she about?"

The captain asked, "Who are you watching?"

She didn't answer. She was too busy wondering why Mr. Brock was interested in Della's pearls.

"Ah, the race." The captain turned, craning his neck to see.

Madeline could hear the slapping pace of the pack as they thundered off. Could smell the feverish excitement of the crowd cheering their wagered favorites to victory.

She saw Wardton leap from the rig and dash away.

A tiny flash of light. The diamond. Madeline caught her breath. *He has the necklace!* She could not be certain, but, yes, she was certain. She must follow him, for in seconds he would be lost in this crowd.

Without pausing to explain, she grabbed the captain's arm and towed the amazed man along with her, thinking that if anyone should ask, she could say she had taken the notion to see the race at close range.

In any case it did not matter. She had to catch up with Wardton, and she needed Titus along for protection.

There, just ahead of them, was Wardton. He had slowed his pace. Perhaps she had been mistaken. He did not act as though he had stolen anything.

"Is something wrong?" Titus asked in a cautious tone.

"Of course not."

"Walking rather fast for a stroll, aren't we?"

She threw him an exasperated look as he guided her around a canvas tent, secluding them from onlookers.

Madeline pointed to where Wardton stood lingering at another of the voluminous tents. She doubted he knew of their presence. Whispering, she said, "Mr. Wardton has snatched Della's pearl necklace. We cannot let him out of our sight."

Titus looked dubious, then he seemed to forget

about her as he focused his attention on Wardton. A smile curved his mouth as he turned back to her. "What will Priscilla Milson's mother say?" Then he burst out laughing.

Madeline pressed her fingers over his lips. "Hush, don't you know I'm serious?" Slowly she removed her hand, trying to ignore her response to the warm brush of his mouth.

"He's a rounder, but I doubt he's the type to follow the racetrack committing robberies."

Annoyed, she tried explaining. "He was sitting directly behind Della and Mr. Brock. Before the race started, I saw Della give her necklace to Brock. During the clamor of the race, Wardton darted into the crowd. With the pearls. And if he didn't take them, something is definitely going on. Why should he run away like that?"

Titus narrowed his gaze, as if mulling over what she had told him.

"You are right to doubt me. Who in his right mind would believe that tale?" That was the problem, no one in England was in his right mind, including her.

She spun around, prepared to chase Wardton, but he had vanished. "He's gone."

"We should never have let him out of our sight," Titus said.

"How astute of you," Madeline murmured, her voice dripping with ice.

They pressed on around the other side of the tent. The crowd swelled and pushed them back. "We should have gone the other way," Madeline said. "We'll never find him in this wild mob."

Madeline felt conspicuous as few females lingered, scattered as they were among the male watchers.

Titus must have been thinking along those lines. "I don't like the looks some of these gentlemen are directing our way. This last day of the races has, in the past, gained a reputation of fistfights and abductions." He clamped his arm around her waist, glaring at some young ruffians. "We had better start back."

On returning to the trees, they found only a pacing Francesca. "Where is everyone?" Titus asked.

"Grandma'am and your mother have taken Della back to the Grange. Her pearl necklace is missing and the poor child is in hysterics."

"And Mr. Brock?" Madeline asked. She noted his cabriolet stood waiting; a young boy held the horse. "Where is he?"

Francesca allowed Titus to help her into her carriage. "The men have all gone off somewhere, except the earl. He left with Della. I have been waiting here, hoping you two would arrive any minute. I cannot imagine why you ran off like that."

They waited for no other information. With a few pence, Titus recruited the boy holding Brock's cabriolet, promising him a larger sum later. He instructed the Esmere footmen to ready the horses for Lady Rowe's carriage, but to wait until he came back before setting out. He handed Madeline into the smaller rig and they wheeled off, searching the mob again.

The narrow roadway teemed with racegoers, and Titus, with the eager help of their young groom, had to alight, calm the mare, and walk her round the mob at the victory circle. Just beyond, he thought he recognized Fredricks's tall figure and Wardton's blond head. Back in the driver's seat, he elbowed Madeline. "Up ahead there. It looks like they're heading for the tavern."

At the improvised tavern, Titus found Brock and Fredricks on the edge of the loop, but no Wardton.

He jumped from the rig, handed Madeline down, and commanded, "Stay here." Their hireling held the horse.

"My good man," Brock said, "surely you do not bring Miss Smythe here, among these rowdy gentlemen?"

Ignoring him, Titus grabbed Fredricks's cravat and demanded, "Where is Nicholas Wardton?" Any child could see the younger man was soused, but Titus was in no mood to be cordial to a drunkard.

Winking at Madeline, Fredricks said, "Ah, Miss Smythe with the honeyed voice that matches the color of her hair. She is a lady in her own right, you know." He stared, glassy-eyed. "Francesca has town bronze, and Della is the local beauty in these parts, but Miss Smythe's charm has a foreign flavor, as a fine wine slipped onto shore by the 'gentlemen,' something quite out of the ordinary you understand."

Titus clenched his jaw. How well he understood.

Whatever else Fredricks would have uttered was cut short. Titus plunged his fist forward, clipping him a forceful facer.

Fredricks dropped to his knees, blood pouring from his nose.

There came a thudding blow to the back of Titus's head. He tried to maintain steadiness, tried lifting his eyelids, but could do neither. His world went hazy as he heard Madeline yell, "Not him. Wardton's the culprit!"

13

Titus opened his eyes to find Madeline kneeling on the ground beside him, with a crowd of rough-looking racetrackers pushing in for a closer look. "Help me up. This is not my favorite position."

On his feet again, he decided he wasn't seriously hurt and Madeline looked as though she had come to no obvious harm.

"Uh." She cleared her throat. "We must hurry."

"Hurry? Someone just slammed me with a brick." He slanted her a suspicious look.

"*I* didn't hit you. Mr. Brock did."

"Brock?" He scanned the onlookers. "Where is Fredricks?"

She gestured to where Fredricks stood leaning against the rig.

Titus grabbed him and demanded, "What do you know about this deal?"

Fredricks stared at Madeline, frowning; the dwindling sunlight glinted on his bloodstained shirtfront. He whipped away from Titus. "I knew nothing of Brock's plan."

Titus regarded him with a skeptical glare. "I have a feeling you know more than you're telling."

Madeline warned, "I don't think we should talk about it at present." With a small wave of her hand, she indicated the watchers.

She was right; they had an audience with many interested locals among the listeners. But at the moment he could care less. He felt like shouting but kept his voice level. After all, he was a gentleman, an army officer. Hell, what did that matter? First, he was a man. A man who had been knocked unconscious in front of his ladylove. He propelled her toward the cabriolet. "Come on, you," he yelled at Fredricks, who meekly followed.

"What's your name?" Titus grumbled at the groom.

"Jem."

He snorted, every male servant in the county claimed the name of Jem. "The hell it is. If you want payment, you'd better tell."

"Harry, sir. I'm the eggman's boy." Bowing, he leaped nimbly onto the rig.

Titus climbed up beside him and indicated the reins to Fredricks. "Think you can handle the ribbons?"

As he had no choice, Fredricks nodded and pressed the mare to a trot.

"You are in a black mood, Captain, and I cannot blame you," Madeline said, turning in the seat to speak to him. "As I said, Brock hit you. I screamed that he had attacked the wrong man. While you lay motionless on the ground, Wardton crept out from behind the tavern. He argued fiercely with Brock and Fredricks." She paused, staring at Fredricks as if expecting him to comment. "Then Wardton gave the necklace to Brock and those two thieves left together."

"Brock and Wardton, you mean?"

She nodded. Harry's head bobbed up and down as he agreed with all that she said.

Fredricks, sobered now, backed up her story.

"Not one gentleman came forward to assist in any way. I thought of going for help, but I couldn't leave you lying there on the ground." She hesitated, then continued, "You were in danger."

By this time they reached the barn where Titus had stabled his mount. "Damn thoughtful of you," he drawled, rubbing the knot on the back of his head.

Madeline rode back to the Grange with Fredricks in the cabriolet. Titus led the way on horseback, and Francesca's carriage covered the rear.

Jaimie met them at the door, his eyes widening at sight of Fredricks's swollen nose and bloody cravat. "What happened? Did you find the pearls?"

"No," Titus growled, "and it's not likely we will."

In the drawing room, Lady Hampden sat flanking Della on one side, Grandma'am on the other.

Their polite manners forbade comment on Fredricks's sorry condition, but Grandma'am clucked her disapproval.

Neither Madeline nor Titus had told Francesca anything, and she was as shocked as the older ladies when Titus said to Della, "The pearls are not lost, but stolen. We have had a thief in our midst."

As the tale of Wardton's snatching of the necklace unfolded, Madeline watched the occupants of the room. She thought it odd that Della was all tears when eyes were upon her, but when the attention switched elsewhere, Della appeared to listen intently. This was especially true when Titus turned to her and said, "Madeline chased after Wardton and later saw him hand the necklace over to Brock."

"What a piece of impertinence," Grandma'am grumbled. "I never did trust him."

The captain was much more vivid with what he thought of Wardton, as well as Brock, and with the picture of what he'd like to do to the scoundrels. "How did he get his hands on the necklace is what I'd like to know."

Della's teary gasp rocked the room. "Just before the race, I was sitting with Mr. Brock in his cabriolet. Nicky Wardton was there, too, and . . . many people were all around." She drew in a wavering breath. "Mr. Brock asked if I would take off the pearls only for a minute; he wanted to examine the diamond."

"I wager he did at that," Titus said sarcastically.

"I released the clasp and we studied the design together, but when the race started, I—"

"Did Brock leave during the race?" Titus asked.

"No, but when the horses finished, the pearls were gone. He helped me look everywhere."

Madeline cleared her throat in the quiet pause. "Wardton was on the rig, behind Della, where a groom would ride. I saw him dart away. It was so sudden, and in the middle of the race." She deliberately left out the part about seeing the diamond; who would believe she caught a flash of it from a distance? "I suspected he was up to no good, and I followed him, dragging Captain Rhodes along with me."

She turned to Fredricks. "Now, I wonder, Mr. Fredricks, if you were the gentleman set to occupy us ladies so we would notice nothing unusual."

All eyes suddenly gazed at Fredricks, as he was known to them as Brock's constant companion.

Jaimie's face darkened as he pointed a finger at him. "Wouldn't be surprised if you were in on the rackety business, bloody nose and all."

No one shushed the earl, instead they looked as though they wanted to heap it on themselves.

"Who jabbed you in the face, Fredricks?" Jaimie asked, his voice a deadly whisper.

Titus stepped in front of Jaimie. "Drop it, there are ladies present."

The room erupted with everyone's own conjectures then, all of them speaking at once. Titus lit a cigar and took a long drag on it.

Madeline stared at him. "Do you smoke?"

"I do now." And he blew a cloud of foul-smelling smoke into the air.

Grandma'am insisted they call the constable.

"No!" Della's voice rose above the rest, and

when she spoke again, it was soft, yet adamant. "No more scandal for this family."

Not one person dared override her decision, either. It was her predicament, her home, her pearls.

Titus faced Fredricks and said in a low voice charged with threat, "I think you had better tell all you know of this crime."

Fredricks's arrogant assurance crumpled. He sank onto the settee, his hands dangling between his knees, and confessed that Brock had done the deed before, at other racetracks. "But I swear, I have never taken part in the theft. Brock has always managed to find someone willing to do the dirty work."

"How can you say you've never taken part?" Madeline demanded. "You ride with him, and follow the tracks as his companion. That makes you an accomplice, even if not intentionally."

Casting a look of disgust Fredricks's way, Jaimie suggested, "We can nab Brock when he comes to fetch his rig."

"That's not likely," Fredricks said, glancing sideways at Francesca. "Rig's mine." He shrugged at Francesca's questioning whoop. "On credit."

"You are an authentic accomplice!" she yelled. "His driver, his partner. Ohhh, Titus, you were so right about Vincent and his influence." In a swish of black-and-white stripes, Francesca crossed the room and stood glaring at her nephew. "I think the British army might be the very solution here."

"You mean join up?" Fredricks squeaked.

"She can afford to buy you a handsome commission," Titus said, with a rather malicious grin. "If she chooses."

Dusk fell, cook served a light meal, a storm blew in, and still Vincent Brock did not return to the Grange.

"He isn't fool enough to come back here," Madeline said.

"And we all know it," Titus agreed. "He is this minute on his way to sell the goods and if even Wardton receives his share, I shall be surprised."

Della fell into Lady Hampden's arms, tears running down her face.

"Hush, Della, you are driving us to distraction," Madeline pleaded. "Be glad that is all you have lost. Only the necklace."

Then it was Grandma'am's turn to gasp.

Titus growled under his breath. "Have you no control over your mouth?" *His* mouth was a disapproving line.

"I was speaking of the matching earrings." She glared at Titus while the others stared at the pear-shaped diamonds on Della's ears.

"They are Madeline's," Della said. "Her mother gave them to her."

"Oh, what does it matter?" Madeline held her temper, waiting three seconds before saying, "The pearls are gone. Della does not wish to pursue the situation. Allow it to rest." She turned on her heels and headed for the stairs, announcing over her shoulder, "I'm going to bed."

It wasn't until the next morning when Madeline went down to breakfast and found Francesca alone in the dining room that she discovered what had happened next. Titus had marched Fredricks upstairs to one of the spare rooms and launched an upbraiding that Fredricks would not soon forget.

"They stayed the night and argued during most of it. Titus declared he would not allow Abel out of his sight until Bradford returned and was told about the necklace. He suspects Brad will seek the constable.

"As soon as Bradford and Almira arrive, I shall apologize for the trouble my nephew and *distant* cousin have caused, then I am delivering Abel to his parents. That task scares me; I'm not sure I can handle it."

"Where is he this morning?" Madeline shuddered; she couldn't even say his name.

"Sleeping, I think. As well as Della. She has not come down."

Madeline simply could not concentrate on the conversation. Even before Francesca told her Titus had stayed the night, she had sensed him in the house. From the first day she walked into Esmere Grange and set eyes on him, he had entangled her in his life. Correction, her own fantasies were responsible for the entanglement.

The solution was for her to leave. But first, she intended to finish what she had started. "Do you agree that the best thing is to see Jaimie and Della betrothed as quickly as possible?"

Francesca hesitated, studying Madeline over her cup of coffee. "I'm not sure, Madeline. A season in London would do so much toward smartening up the girl. She's lacking in sophistication, and is only now trying her wings. A woman needs to see for herself how other women perceive the man she loves, just as it is good for the groom to know other men desire his bride."

Madeline was undeterred. "But Jaimie has vowed to speak for her when Uncle Bradford returns. And I intend to encourage them both along those lines."

"I shall fete Della if she comes to me for the season. You, also, but I have the feeling you are planning otherwise." The last was uttered softly with a questioning tone.

Madeline swallowed and met her gaze with directness. "I think I must."

"Were you serious when you told Titus you were thinking of starting a business?"

"Yes, but he didn't think much of the notion."

From her look, neither did Francesca. And Madeline did not volunteer the information that Titus had apologized for his behavior on that evening.

But, she had apologized first.

"Don't be surprised if Della loses interest in Jaimie once she sees London. Temporarily at least."

Madeline smiled. "I think that's what Jaimie fears the most."

"I've quite enjoyed coming home to my old neighborhood," Francesca went on. "Next summer I might open my family's home. I've been thinking about it. It's been years since I've spent any time there."

"Della would love having you near."

"When I was Della's age, I was in love with Bradford. I thought I would die when he married

Almira. Titus forced me to attend the wedding; he knew it was only infatuation. Titus is such a good friend." She shook her head. "It would never have worked between Bradford and me."

Madeline didn't want to listen to this. She was afraid Francesca might confess that her friendship with the captain had developed into love. She glanced at her, fearful she could somehow read her mind, but Francesca only looked back at her in interested silence.

A servant came in to remove the plates, followed by Pixie, who hovered on the threshold. She bobbed her curtsy. "Could you come at once, Miss Smythe?"

"Why, what is it, Pixie? Your voice is trembling."

Pixie advanced into the room, her starched apron rustling. "It's Lady Della. She—she's gone."

Madeline jumped to her feet, overturning her coffee.

Pixie thrust a note into Madeline's hands and burst into sobs.

"Dear God in Heaven," Francesca whispered, folding her hands at her throat. "What has happened now?"

Madeline quickly scanned the letter. "She is meeting Wardton at the Green Dragon. They planned it. There was no robbery. They planned this whole hoax! It was the only way, don't you see? Neither of them had enough of their own money to travel far." Della's behavior yesterday in the carriage was suddenly clear to her. "That's why she wore her pearls and why she was so fidgety. Remember, yesterday before noon when we started out?"

Francesca stared. "You don't mean elope? Della has more sense. She is bound to be around somewhere. She could not leave home without a horse or carriage, and Titus left strict orders with the stable to report anyone near the house."

Madeline traded a conspiratorial look with Pixie. "The eggman. Go, quickly, and see if he's been here."

Jaimie had just been admitted into the corridor with his mother and Grandma'am in tow when Madeline and Francesca rushed out of the dining room.

With no preamble, Madeline shushed their greetings and gestured for them to follow her into the drawing room. Hesitating for only a second, she met their curious gazes, then blundered into a hasty explanation.

For minutes no one spoke. It was too much to comprehend. Waving the piece of paper, Madeline said, "Brock is to exchange the necklace for cash. She says, 'We shall take the money to wed and to live on until Nicky has inherited what is rightfully his.'"

"Nicky has no inheritance that I know of," Jaimie croaked. He brushed a hand through his hair.

He looked petrified with fear, but mainly he looked terrible. Bags under his bloodshot eyes, dark circles around them. Madeline didn't pity him; she'd had a bad night herself.

Grandma'am's voice had an edge to it as she said, "A diversion, that is what Della needs. The girl has been cooped up here all her life. No wonder she tries unnatural escapades."

Francesca flinched at such obvious criticism of her supervision.

Madeline, impatient with them, spoke directly to Jaimie, "What she needs is to be brought safely home. How are we to accomplish that?"

Instead of listening to the plan concocted afterward, Madeline thought of Titus Rhodes. She could draw on her own grit and backbone; she had that and could probably manage, but in this scandalous situation, she needed Titus. She wished for his unyielding courage in the face of possible danger.

She would have to ask for his help.

Alone in the billiards room, Titus chewed on one of Bradford's cigars and wished his friend were here. He was tired of this protector role. With five women, he was grossly outnumbered.

In the past few weeks, he had asked himself what he was doing back here in Leaside in any case. He should be on bivouac somewhere, or in a map room listening to consultations. Slowly, he'd realized his healing was complete, the leg pains would undoubtably always be there, and his rememberings. Yet, it was time he moved on.

He thought about Abel Fredricks and Nicky Wardton, shuddering to think Jaimie could have turned out exactly like them.

And for the hundredth time since waking, he thought about Madeline Smythe. He had finally found a woman he wanted to spend the rest of his life with. He admired her exquisite beauty and gentle-heartedness. She had a sense of family loyalty and was the type who could face whatever the future held. She was pluck to the backbone, and he was scared to death she would reject him.

He scrubbed the stubble on his chin. Yesterday he had come within an inch of proposing.

There was a rap on the door. It opened and he looked around at Madeline.

"I'm glad you're still here." She stood with her back stiff, hands knotted by her sides. Then she swept curling strands of that honey-gold hair behind her ears and he saw how nervous and frightened she was, how vulnerable.

It was probably a feminine enticement. He should know. He'd watched her teach Della enough of those little acts. "Well?"

"We have a problem."

She smelled like lavender and oranges. "You're speaking about yesterday when I stood around spying on you?"

She blinked at him. "I beg your pardon?"

His breath was foul, he still had on yesterday's clothes. He must look like a pitiful hunk of male. "I was ready to declare my love for you. No, to be precise, how *much* I love you. Ready to ask you to spend the rest of your life with me. Romantic nonsense," he said, gritting his teeth, angry with himself for blurting out like that. "Who wished you on me, I would like to know?"

She bristled. "I came to you for help. You are the one person I thought with sense enough to know what to do."

"What are you raving about? Since when do you need help?"

"Nicholas Wardton has abducted Della."

"The devil he has. That sapsucker hasn't the brains to abduct a woman. Is he our thief, or not?"

"The devil and Della, do you hear?"

There was a sober light in her eyes, and he finally realized the seriousness of the matter. She told him of Della's note.

"We will need Jaimie."

"He's at the stable now."

"Here?" He pitched his cigar into the grate. "Right, horseback. It's the fastest way of travel. Do you know their direction?"

"We can only guess. Her letter mentions the Green Dragon."

"In that event, the whole county will know their whereabouts." He groaned. "Is nothing simple?"

He heard footsteps. In the gilt-edged alcove leading to the music room there stood Francesca, his mother, and Grandma'am. His neck flamed as he realized he had most likely had an audience through his whole damnable declaration.

"Not on horseback, and not the curricle, Titus. You must go in the closed carriage to bring her back. Her reputation is at stake. We must keep the affair as private as possible." This speech from his mother.

Then he noticed the maid, Esther, standing there with a bag, holding Madeline's heavy cape. "What's this?"

"Surely you do not think we could allow you and Jaimie to fetch her without another female along?"

He regarded Madeline with a skeptical stare. "No."

Madeline didn't hesitate. "Yes, I forced her into this mess, and I shall help extract her."

"Consider yourself lucky we all don't wish to follow you," Grandma'am insisted.

He laughed sarcastically, flinging out his arms. "In any case, I don't know why I have even been consulted. The matronly army of Leaside has spoken."

14

Madeline's mind whirled. Romantic nonsense. What did he mean by that? She had hurriedly dressed in her gray traveling dress with matching pelisse and hat, her curly tresses smoothed into a knot at the back of her head. Already a few spirals escaped about her face.

"Miss Smythe!" Pixie came running across the cobblestoned drive. She gave a quick bob in the general direction of all, and breathlessly exclaimed, "You should come onto the eggman at the wide bend in the road, the place of the high cliff." She leaned close to whisper in Madeline's ear, "Cook says he most certainly has news of Della."

Madeline tried to swallow her fear, fervently praying that Della was safe and had not committed some irrevocable act, damning her reputation. But she thought it not surprising that Della had managed to outwit them.

As the carriage approached the so-called bend in the road, the eggman stood up in his wagon and waved them on. "Hollingsford Farm!" he shouted, and the earl's team thundered on by.

Madeline sat facing the brothers and their determined faces. The captain's concern seemed more like a father's for a daughter's safety. Jaimie's came near to outrage. With himself? Or with Della for running away with Wardton?

"What could she have been thinking?" Jaimie said, trading a worried look with Titus. "Wardton is a regular rakehell."

"You should have thought of that the first time you brought him home with you," Titus answered.

Jaimie took only slight notice of his brother's surly tone. "I thought Della had accepted an invitation to visit Lady Rowe for the season starting in September. Wardton is the last man I would think—"

Forgetting momentarily her own silent turmoil, Madeline asked Jaimie, "Did you give her reason to believe you cared for her?"

Jaimie gave her a less than tolerant look.

"If a man loves a woman, he should not complain of her," Madeline said, conscious of the captain's gaze on her.

Sputtering, Jaimie declared, "She knows I care for her."

"But have you *told* her?" Madeline leaned forward; it was difficult to keep eye contact with him, for the carriage bounced so at such high speed. "Have you never kissed her?"

A flush crept up the earl's cheeks. "I refuse to answer such a question."

Madeline could not keep back a wide grin. "I understand. You do not wish to admit to such improper behavior, but where I come from a kiss is a declaration of serious intention. You might remind Della of your . . . intimacy. Especially if she kissed you back."

The captain stiffened and threw her a warning look, but Jaimie answered this with an enlightening dawning in his eyes.

"Much of this is your own fault," Titus told Jaimie. "You had a chance to speak for her weeks ago. First you wanted to marry, then you declared for the bachelor's life. Now are you back to marriage? Do you know your own mind?"

"Let me see now," Jaimie grumbled, directing a steely gaze at Titus. "You jabbed Fredricks in the nose?"

Titus merely nodded.

"A man does not commit violence for no good reason." Jaimie gave Madeline a penetrating stare, then turned back to Titus and drawled, "Thought as much that day we found you alone at Seascape."

Madeline blinked and looked away.

Jaimie persisted. "Why else would you have trounced him? Not that I don't think he earned it."

At the moment, Titus's face was more forbidding than on the day he'd hit Fredricks.

Irritated that they spoke as though she were not planted right in front of them, Madeline would not interrupt. She was fascinated with this subtle dialogue between them, suspecting it was their usual mode of conversation. Parry an attack, then return with a quick riposte.

How sly they thought they were. Jaimie was claiming that Titus loved her? Titus had said so himself. Now Jaimie confirmed it.

She spared another glance at Titus, giving him a questioning stare.

He sent a quizzical look right back at her.

A somewhat quiet man, the captain was one of strong character and could easily change from austere and wise to a man full of humor. At the moment he took on an air that clearly said, "Do not trifle with me." Then he commenced explaining to his brother that the sale of the lower portion of Hampden Estates, combined with the profits from his future factory on the Hollingsford Farm lands, would produce enough revenue to repair the Hampden finances. "There is a gentleman in London, a tradesman, waiting for your decision."

Jaimie's mouth worked as he appeared to think over this new development. Obviously, this was the first he had heard of the plan. "Then it won't be necessary that I wed to save us from losing everything?"

Titus shook his head. "I previously informed Miss Smythe of this, and I believe she understands the practical nature of it."

Madeline did not give him the satisfaction of a comment. This was clearly a matter between the two brothers.

"And since you have made no offers," Titus paused, scowling at Madeline, "there can be no claim of a broken contract."

"What of Della's heart?" Madeline asked.

At her irate glare, the captain shrugged, and Jaimie stared glumly out the window.

Dead silence reigned inside the earl's grand carriage until they drew in at the gates of Hollingsford Farm.

Struck with the sad aura surrounding the pile of old gray stones, Madeline wondered if pulling down the crumbling house overrun with vines was part of the plan for erection of the factory.

Inside, they found Della sitting on a lone table in the old mansion's empty corridor, dust motes swirling in the light from the open door.

She stood and faced them, her shoulders back, her face pale, but calm. "I rode here in the eggman's cart. I intended to meet Nicholas Wardton, but I knew when I started out this morning that I could not go to the Green Dragon and flaunt our scheme to all who saw us there."

Madeline smiled. "How glad we are." In her mind, Della looked and spoke exactly like the countess she was destined to be.

"He wouldn't have been there anyway," Della whispered.

"How gallant that the earl has come in search of you," Madeline said, hoping Della could read her secret smile. She elbowed Jaimie, who stood stiffer than a fence post. He looked as though he wanted to say something, but an inner struggle marred his expression. She caught unsettling glances exchanged between him and Della. They were clearly embarrassed and uncomfortable with each other. "Perhaps Della and I should go into another part of the house where we might speak in private."

"I recognize a hint when I hear one." The angry lights in Jaimie's eyes flashed as he walked out the door, pivoted, and stalked back to stand in front of Della. "I have a right to be here."

Della's voice was raw. "Why?"

"I care about you." He heaved a heavy sigh. "What possessed you to do such a thing?"

Sullenly, she answered, "Because Nicky convinced me he wanted me, and only me."

Jaimie could not hide the pained expression on his face. "Wanted you, yes, I am sure he did."

Madeline stepped in between them. "What you want, Della, is a man to love you, and to care for you, not one who wants only what he can gain."

"The necklace?"

"And there is your fortune, which I suspect he was after all along."

"I—I wasn't going to go through with it. I really detest Nicky's mustache, but Abel said, he said—"

Madeline embraced her. "I'm sure I can guess what *he* said."

"I thought you enamoured of Fredricks," Jaimie said. "He certainly gave you enough opportunity."

"More than one of you ladies fell under his spell," Titus interjected.

Madeline raised her eyebrows. "Please, give us credit for a bit of sense."

Titus cleared his throat. "You must realize, Della girl, that Brock really had no intention of handing the money over to Wardton. A man like him? He will keep every ounce of it."

With his gaze only for Della, Jaimie implored, "What were you thinking?"

Della struggled to overcome tears. The truth was suddenly clear to Madeline. In an attempt to pay Jaimie back for what she had been calling his ill treatment of her, Della had wound herself in a web of revenge. That must surely be the reason why she had been so uncomfortable in Jaimie's presence.

She loves him, Madeline tried to communicate to Titus.

"You are meddling again," Titus warned in a low voice.

"I am not," she protested.

Now they had seen for themselves that Della was safe, the captain's mood changed to one of an amused bystander. "I suggest we leave them alone so they can work things out on their own."

Before they crossed the threshold, Madeline caught a glimpse of Della's face as Jaimie blurted out, "When we are married, you cannot go haring around like some foxhound."

Both Madeline and Titus halted on hearing this blunt and unromantic offer. Madeline would have turned back, but Titus grasped her wrist, pulling her behind the door and closing it firmly. "Let them go at it."

She threw him an aggravated glance. "That was characteristic of Jaimie, his usual brusque speech."

"It is proof he truly cares for her. I remind you, he knew before we arrived that he did not have to marry her to save the family estates. And the evidence leans to the probability that they have discussed marriage recently. Now if we can only live through their future ardent exploits."

He grasped her about the waist and propelled

her outside into the warm, breezy day. "I have spent considerable time and money arranging matters so they do not *have* to marry. Let them go their separate ways for now. It is best. By next spring they will be wed. I'll wager my gray on it."

The sound of the other couple's angry voices echoed through the timbers of the old manor. "Will their bickering never cease?"

"I think not." Titus laughed. "They've been at it since the cradle." He took her hand and kissed her bare wrist above her short leather gloves. "All is well, never fear."

"At length, you will probably be glad to see the last of my meddling when I'm gone."

"A lady with a plan to go into business cannot give up and leave. Am I to rescue you by making an offer?"

Choosing his favorite phrase, she said, "I think not. We shall find a way out of this. You care for Francesca and I could never play the second choice."

"Francesca? What has she to do with anything?"

"That night at the Grange, the first evening Brock and Fredricks arrived, when you chastised her about Mr. Brock. I thought you jealous of him."

"If I was jealous that evening, it was because the gentlemen sat comfortably lounging, their gazes riveted on the three beauties who surrounded them. One honey-gold lady in particular."

His expression sent shivers of excitement down Madeline's back. Ever since the kiss she now referred to as the Seascape kiss, she had resisted the urge to draw him with feminine enticement. She had resisted confusing him as he had her. But this morning in the billiards room, his declaration had worked its magic, had clicked off spontaneous giddiness inside her. Madeline Rose Smythe, proper Canadian miss, fought bubbles of laughter deep down in her stomach. "You guessed my reason for questioning Jaimie about kissing Della?"

"I wondered if you were about to confess your own sins."

A soft laugh burst from her.

"The thoughts behind that tide of giggles?" he asked, a hint of amusement underscoring his words.

"That day at Seascape when you kissed me, and I kissed you. My life changed afterward."

"How?"

"I knew I could never go back to my former self. I forgot how to be practical, and wise, and *Canadian*. I lived in an air of mystery I'd never known before, squandering my time sending you secretive glances, and tingling when you answered them with looks that muddled my every thought." She spoke haltingly, studying his reaction.

"Shocking," he whispered, slipping his arms about her.

She knew instinctively the look he bestowed on her was the one pirates of old had perfected. The one with which they had seduced unsuspecting maidens. A delicious and deep certainty rippled through her. A sureness so intense it hurt her stomach.

She wound her arms around him.

"Brave of you to indulge in such closeness with a man who hasn't shaved since yesterday," he mumbled in a caressing voice.

"Never mind. I suppose I shall grow used to your whiskers."

He kissed her then with a sudden fierceness that left her with an unwavering knowledge that their parting could leave a hole in her being. One that would never go away.

"Romantic nonsense. Could you explain the phrase?" Madeline asked when she could breathe again.

"I hear a warning in your voice that tells me I shall eternally regret those rash words."

There was a teasing glint in his eyes that muddled Madeline's thoughts even now.

"I had declared myself," he said, "and did not, at the time, intend to do so again."

How could she have fallen in love with such an unpredictable man as this?

"The pain in my leg will not allow us a trip to the border," he said after another of those vigorous kisses. "Would a special license and a quick ceremony here at home do?"

"A special license." She sighed. "That sounds the quickest route."

Confusion prevailed on the day Uncle Bradford's coach came lumbering up the drive. As soon as Aunt Almira heard about the theft of the pearls and of Della's precipitate flight, she swooned and had to be carried to bed. Uncle Bradford swore several oaths, and made frightening threats. But for all his blustering, he didn't accomplish one thing except for soothing his wife.

No one seemed in the least surprised when Titus announced that he and Madeline planned to wed. In fact, the occupants of the connecting estates received the news with equanimity.

Grandma'am smacked Titus on the back, saying, "I thought as much."

They were married outdoors on the garden terrace at the Grange, the breezes warm and soft with airy white clouds floating out to sea. Lady Hampden spent the time with tears in her eyes, and Grandma'am sat regally nodding her head in rapt approval. Della clustered with the ladies and ignored all attention from any male who looked her way.

"That attitude will disappear once she arrives at Francesca's," Titus whispered to Madeline.

Their world narrowed to just the two of them as darkness fell and they drove in Titus's curricle to Seascape cottage. They planned to live there for the next few weeks with only Sheridan and Esther in attendance.

On the day following the quiet ceremony, the Esmeres, Lady Hampden, Della, and Grandma'am made their way to London to visit with Lady Francesca Rowe for the little season. After their departure, Jaimie glumly revealed, "Della has promised to give me her answer after she returns from London."

"Sensible lady," Madeline said.

Jaimie's lips tightened, "I suppose I should prepare myself for a whirlwind courtship."

Titus warned, "Your main problem is to see she accepts no other offers."

Wherein Jaimie gave a derisive snort and mounted his horse. Urging the roan to a gallop, he chased after the disappearing carriages.

At Seascape Cottage another week passed. After dinner one evening, Madeline read an entertaining letter aloud to her new husband. "From Francesca, darling. Listen to what she says about Vincent Brock."

Before arriving here, Bradford consulted with the local constablary, but he insists we must let it rest. Madeline glanced at Titus, who lounged in a wing chair before the red coals in the grate. "She speaks of the pearls, of course."

Bradford says Vincent Brock will never change, and we are well rid of him. He assures us Vincent will receive his comeuppance in due time.

"Did you hear, Titus?"

The captain yawned and, without opening his eyes, nodded. "Had a long talk with Bradford before our wedding, when everyone was bustling about with the flowers and chairs. He's so besotted over the possibility of a forthcoming heir, he could care less about the family jewels."

Madeline dropped the letter in her lap, giddiness threatening to explode. "You don't mean?"

Wide awake now, he smiled. "Almira is madder than a wet cat because she'll miss the regular season. To assuage her ire, or smooth their relations—I don't know which—he agreed to haul the entire family for the little season. Otherwise, I do not believe he could have been persuaded to go to town. Not with someone like Francesca willing to sponsor Della."

"So there might be an Esmere to carry on the family name, and Almira will be too busy with a new babe to bother so much with Della's doings."

He laughed at her astonished face. "All that accomplished without you having to raise a hand."

Ignoring the book she sailed in his direction, he sent her an intimate smile.

Picking up the note again, she continued, "Grandma'am and your mother are taking on a good deal of shopping excursions."

"Nothing unusual about Mother shopping, but Grandma'am?"

Madeline laughed. "The truth is, they don't trust Almira's choice of gowns for her daughter."

He beckoned to her. "Join me. We have the cottage all to ourselves for another week before we must travel to London to negotiate with the factory owners. Let us not waste a moment of our time."

The forgotten letter slipped to the floor. He waited while she nestled on his lap, folding his arms around her and kissing her pink mouth and the delicate structure of her jaw and chin. He studied the long lashes framing passion-filled eyes. In their long nights together, he'd found his wife had a zest for adventure that surprised his soldier's hide. To think he had worried about whether the nine years' difference in their ages would matter to her at all.

He brushed the light curls back from her face and said, "The earl's brother is going into trade, and his new wife, establishing a business of her own. We'll set them all on their ears."

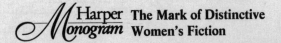

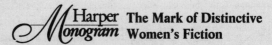